ONLY THE WORTHY

(THE WAY OF STEEL – BOOK ONE)

MORGAN RICE

THE WEIGHT OF HONOR (Book #3)
A FORGE OF VALOR (Book #4)
A REALM OF SHADOWS (Book #5)
NIGHT OF THE BOLD (Book #6)

THE SORCERER'S RING
A QUEST OF HEROES (Book #1)
A MARCH OF KINGS (Book #2)
A FATE OF DRAGONS (Book #3)
A CRY OF HONOR (Book #4)
A VOW OF GLORY (Book #5)
A CHARGE OF VALOR (Book #6)
A RITE OF SWORDS (Book #7)
A GRANT OF ARMS (Book #8)
A SKY OF SPELLS (Book #9)
A SEA OF SHIELDS (Book #10)
A REIGN OF STEEL (Book #11)
A LAND OF FIRE (Book #12)
A RULE OF QUEENS (Book #13)
AN OATH OF BROTHERS (Book #14)
A DREAM OF MORTALS (Book #15)
A JOUST OF KNIGHTS (Book #16)
THE GIFT OF BATTLE (Book #17)

THE SURVIVAL TRILOGY
ARENA ONE: SLAVERSUNNERS (Book #1)
ARENA TWO (Book #2)
ARENA THREE (Book #3)

VAMPIRE, FALLEN
BEFORE DAWN (Book #1)

THE VAMPIRE JOURNALS
TURNED (Book #1)
LOVED (Book #2)
BETRAYED (Book #3)
DESTINED (Book #4)
DESIRED (Book #5)
BETROTHED (Book #6)
VOWED (Book #7)
FOUND (Book #8)
RESURRECTED (Book #9)

The word of the Lord came to me, saying: "Before I formed you in the womb I knew you, before you were born I set you apart; I appointed you as a prophet to the nations."

But I said: "Alas, my Lord, I do not know how to speak; I am too young."

But the Lord said to me, "Do not say, 'I am too young.' Rather, wherever I shall send you, you shall go, and whatever I command you, you shall speak. Do not fear them, for I am with you and will rescue you."

Jeremiah 1:4–7

PART ONE

CHAPTER ONE

Rea sat upright in her simple bed, sweating, awakened by the shrieks that tore through the night. Her heart pounded as she sat in the dark, hoping it was nothing, that it was just another one of the nightmares that had been plaguing her. She gripped the edge of her cheap straw mattress and listened, praying, willing for the night to be silent.

Another shriek came, though, and Rea flinched.

Then another.

They were becoming more frequent—and getting closer.

Frozen in fear, Rea sat there and listened as they neared. Above the sound of the lashing rain there also came the sound of horses, faint at first, then the distinctive sound of swords being drawn. But none were louder than the shrieking.

And then a new sound arose, one which, if possible, was even worse: the crackle of flames. Rea's heart sank as she realized her village was being set ablaze. That could only mean one thing: the nobles had arrived.

Rea jumped from bed, banging her knee against the andirons, her only possession in her simple one-room cottage, and then running from the house. She emerged to the muddy street, into the warm rain of spring, the downpour getting her instantly wet. Yet she did not care. She blinked into the darkness, still trying to shake off her nightmare. All around her, shutters opened, doors opened, and her fellow villagers stepped tentatively from their cottages. They all stood and stared down the single simple road winding into the village. Rea stared with them and in the distance spotted a glow. Her heart sank. It was a spreading flame.

Living here, in the poorest part of the village, hidden behind the twisting labyrinths that wound their way from the main town square, was, at a time like this, a blessing; she would at least be safe back here. Nobody ever came back here, to this poorest part of town, to these ramshackle cottages where only the servants lived, where the stink of the streets forced people away. It had always felt like a ghetto that Rea could not get out of.

Yet as she watched the flames lick the night, Rea was relieved, for the first time, to live back here, hidden. The nobles would never bother trying to navigate the labyrinthine streets and back alleys that led here. There was nothing to pillage here, after all.

Rea knew that was why her destitute neighbors merely stood outside their cottages, not panicking, but merely watching. That was why, too, none of them attempted to run to the aid of the villagers in the town center, those rich folk who had looked down upon them their entire lives. They owed them nothing. The poor were safe back here, at least, and they would not risk their lives to save those who had treated them as less than nothing.

And yet, as Rea studied the night, she was baffled to see the flames getting closer, the night brighter. The glow was clearly spreading, creeping its way toward her. She blinked, wondering if her eyes were deceiving her. It didn't make any sense: the marauders seemed to be heading her way.

The shrieks grew louder, she was certain of it, and she flinched as suddenly flames erupted hardly a hundred feet before her, emerging from the labyrinthine streets. She stood there, stunned. They were coming this way. But why?

Hardly had she finished the thought than a galloping warhorse thundered into the square, ridden by a fierce knight donned in all-black armor. His visor was lowered, his helmet drawn to a sinister point. Wielding a halberd, he looked like a messenger of death.

Barely had he entered the square than he lowered his halberd on the back of a portly old man who tried to run. The man hadn't even time to scream before the halberd severed his head.

Lightning filled the skies and thunder struck, the rain intensifying, as a dozen more knights burst into the square. One of them bore a standard. It glowed in the light of the torches, yet Rea could not make out the insignia.

Chaos ensued. Villagers panicked, turned and ran, shrieking, some running back into their cottages by some remote instinct, slipping in the mud, a few fleeing through back alleys. Yet even these did not get far before flying spears found a place in their backs. Death, she knew, would spare no one on this night.

Rea did not try to run. She merely stepped back calmly, reached inside the door of her cottage, and drew a sword, a long sword given to her ages ago, a beautiful work of craftsmanship. The sound of it being drawn from its scabbard made her heart beat faster. It was a masterpiece, a weapon she had no right to own, handed down by her father. She didn't know how he himself had gained it.

Rea walked slowly and resolutely into the center of the town square, the only one of her villagers brave enough to stand their ground, to face these men. She, a frail seventeen-year-old girl, and she alone, had the courage to fight in the face of fear. She didn't know where her courage came from. She wanted to flee, yet something deep inside her forbade it. Something within her had always driven her to face her fears, whatever the odds. It was not that she did not feel terror; she did. It was that another part of her allowed her to function in the face of it. Challenged her to be stronger than it.

Rea stood there, hands trembling, but forcing herself to stay focused. And as the first horse galloped for her, she raised her sword, stepped up, leaned low, and chopped off the horse's legs.

It pained her to do it, to maim this beautiful animal; she had, after all, spent most of her life caring for horses. But the man had raised his spear, and she knew her survival was at stake.

The horse shrieked an awful sound that she knew would stay with her the rest of her days. It fell to the ground, face-planting in the dirt and throwing its knight. The horses behind it rode into it, stumbling and crashing down in a pile around her.

In a cloud of dust and chaos, Rea spun and faced them all, ready to die here.

A single knight, in all-white armor, riding a white horse that was different from the others, suddenly charged right for her. She raised her sword to strike again, but this knight was too fast. He moved like lightning. Barely had she raised her sword than he swung his halberd in an upward arc, catching her blade, disarming her. A helpless feeling ran down her arm as her precious weapon was stripped away, sailing in a broad arc through the air and landing in the mud on the far side of the square. It might as well have been a million miles away.

Rea stood there, stunned to find herself defenseless, but most of all confused. That knight's blow had not been meant to kill her. *Why?*

Before she could finish the thought, the knight, still riding, leaned low and grabbed her; she felt his metal gauntlet digging into her chest as he grabbed her shirt with two hands and in a single motion heaved her up onto his horse, seating her before him. She shrieked at the shock of it, landing roughly on his moving horse, planted firmly in front of him, his metal arms wrapped around her, holding her tight. She barely had time to think, much less to breathe, as he held her in a vise. Rea writhed, bucking side to side, but it was no use. He was too strong.

"Stop struggling," he ordered her. "I'm trying to save your life."

Rea wasn't sure she believed him, but even so, she went still. He continued on, galloping right through the village, weaving his way through the tortuous streets and away from her home. Another of the knights approached him, and he raised his sword.

"She's mine," her captor snapped, and the other knight backed off.

"I'm not yours," Rea said, fear growing in her. "I'm not anyone's."

"The peasant wenches do struggle, don't they?" the other knight laughed.

The one who had seized Rea said nothing. They burst out of the village into the countryside, and suddenly, all was quiet. They rode farther and farther from the chaos, from the pillaging, the shrieking, and Rea could not help but feel guilty for her momentary sense of relief to have the world be at peace again. She felt she should have died back there, with her people. Yet as he held her tighter and tighter, she realized her fate might be even worse.

"Please," she struggled to say, finding it hard to get the word out.

But he only held her tighter and galloped faster into the open meadow, up and down rolling hills, in the pouring rain, until they were in a place of utter quiet. It was eerie, so quiet and peaceful here, as if nothing had ever been wrong in the world.

Finally he stopped on a broad plateau high above the countryside, beneath an ancient tree, a tree she instantly recognized. She had sat beneath it many times before.

In one quick motion he dismounted, keeping his grip on her and taking her with him. They landed in the wet grass, rolling, stumbling, and Rea felt winded as his weight landed beside her. She noted as they landed that he could have landed on top of her, could have really hurt her, but chose not to. In fact, he landed in a way that cushioned her fall.

"Who are you?" Rea demanded. "What do you want with me?"

"You wouldn't understand," the knight said, sitting up. Rea couldn't see his face, the white visor on his armor down, only strong, almost violet eyes appearing from behind the slits of his helmet. On his horse she saw that banner again, and this time she got a good look at its insignia: two snakes, wrapped around a moon, a dagger between them, encased in a circle of gold.

He reached for her and Rea flailed, punching his armor. But it was useless. Hers were frail, small hands punching at a suit of metal. She might as well have been punching a boulder.

4

"I don't plan to hurt you," the knight said. "I don't plan to do anything with you, unless you want it of me."

Rea knew what he meant, and froze. She was seventeen. She had been saving herself for the perfect man. She hadn't thought it would be like this. Or had she? Her dream came back to her, the one she had been awakened from, the one she had been having for many moons. She had seen this scene. This tree, this grass, this plateau. This storm. This man.

Somehow, she had foreseen it, and she realized that it had been him she had been waiting for.

"I dreamed of you too," he said. "I dreamed that you were in danger, and I dreamed of what would come from us, together, in this place. If you had stayed with the others, you would have been cut down, no matter how brave you were. Here, we can begin something new, if you want it."

Rea could remember her dreams of this man, and what he had been like. Just the thought of them made her reach up for him.

"Yes," she whispered over the sound of the rain.

His hands went to her dress as he pushed her down to the ground beneath the tree. Rea had never been with a man, but she had seen what was involved with the animals of her village. There was nothing animal about this though. The man above her removed only the bare minimum of his armor, didn't so much as show her his face, but even so, he was gentle with her, and when the moment came, Rea found herself holding onto him tightly.

All too soon, it was done and Rea lay there on the grass, not quite knowing what to do next. She heard the sound of metal as the knight donned his full armor once more. He moved to her, holding something out and squeezing it into her fingers.

She squinted in the rain and was stunned to see he had placed a gold necklace in her hand, a pendant at its end, two snakes wrapped around a moon, a dagger between them.

"I'm not some whore to be paid," she snapped.

"When he is born," he replied, "give this to him, and send him to me."

She looked up at him.

"You're leaving, aren't you?" she said. "Just like that, you're leaving."

"You'll be safe here," he replied, "and if I'm gone too long, there will be people who look for me. It's better if I go."

"Better for who?" Rea shot back. She closed her eyes. Over the sound of the rain, she heard the knight mounting his horse, and became dimly aware of the sound of his riding away.

Rea's eyes grew heavy. She was too exhausted to move as she lay there in the rain. Her heart shattered, she felt sweet sleep coming on and she allowed it to embrace her. Maybe now, at least, the endless dreams would stop.

Before she let sleep claim her, she stared out at the necklace, the emblem. She squeezed it, feeling it in her hand, the gold so thick, thick enough to feed her entire village for a lifetime.

Why had he given it to her? Why hadn't he left her to be killed?

Him, he had said. This hadn't been about her. He'd known she would be pregnant. And he knew it would be a boy.

How?

Suddenly, before sweet sleep took her, it all came rushing back to her. The last piece of her dream.

A boy. She had given birth to a boy. One born of a night of fury and violence.

A boy destined to be king.

CHAPTER TWO

Three Moons Later

Rea stood alone in the forest clearing, in a daze, lost in her own world. She did not hear the stream trickling beneath her feet, did not hear the chirping of the birds in the thick wood around her, did not notice the sunlight shining through the branches, or the pack of deer that watched her close by. The entire world melted away as she stared at only one thing: the veins of the Ukanda leaf that she held in her trembling fingers. She removed her palm from the broad, green leaf, and slowly, to her horror, the color of its veins changed from green to white.

Watching it change was like a knife in her heart.

The Ukanda did not change colors unless the person who touched it was with child.

Rea's world reeled. She lost all sense of time and space as she stood there, her heart pounding in her ears, her hands trembling, and thought back to that fateful night three moons ago when her village had been pillaged, too many of her people killed to count. When *he* had taken her. She reached down and ran her hand over her stomach, feeling the slightest bump, feeling another wave of nausea, and finally, she understood why. She reached down and fingered the gold necklace she'd been hiding around her neck, deep beneath her clothes, of course, so that the others would not see it, and she wondered, for the millionth time, who that knight was.

Try as she did to block them out, his final words rang again and again in her head.

Send him to me.

There came a sudden rustling behind her and Rea turned, startled, to see the beady eyes of Prudence, her neighbor, staring back at her. A fourteen-year-old girl who lost her family in the attack, a busybody who had always been too eager to tattle on anyone, Prudence was the last person Rea wanted to know her news. Rea watched with horror as Prudence's eyes drifted from Rea's hand to the changing leaf, then widened in recognition.

With a glare of disapproval, Prudence dropped her basket of sheets and turned and ran. Rea knew her running off could only mean one thing: she was going to inform the villagers.

Rea's heart sank, and she felt her first wave of fear. The villagers would demand she kill her baby, of course. They wanted no reminder of the nobles' attack. But why did that scare her? Did she really want to keep this child, the byproduct of that violent night?

Rea's fear surprised her, and as she dwelled on it, she realized it was a fear to keep her baby safe. That floored her. Intellectually, she did not want to have it; to do so would put her village at risk. It would only embolden the nobles who had raided. And it would be so easy to lose the baby; she could merely chew the Yukaba root, and with her next bathing, the child would pass.

Yet viscerally, she felt the child inside her, and her body was telling her something that her mind was not: she wanted to keep it. To protect it. It was a child, after all, and one who had been promised to her in her dreams.

Rea, an only child who had never known her parents, who had suffered in this world with no one to love and no one to love her, had always desperately wanted someone to love, and someone to love her back. She was tired of being alone, of being quarantined in the poorest section of the village, of scratching at the dirt for enough to live, doing hard labor from morning to night with no way out. She would never find a man, she knew, given her status; at least, no man she didn't despise. She would likely never have a child other than this.

Rea felt a sudden surge of longing. This might be her only chance, she realized. And now that she was pregnant, she realized she hadn't known how badly she wanted this child. She wanted it more than anything.

Rea began the hike back to her village, on edge, caught up in a swirl of mixed emotions, hardly prepared to face the disapproval she knew would be awaiting her. The villagers would insist there be no surviving issue from the marauders of their town, from the men who had taken everything from them. They wouldn't understand that things had been different with this man; that he had protected her. Rea could hardly blame them; it was a common tactic for marauders to impregnate women in order to dominate and control the villages throughout the kingdom. Sometimes they would even send for the child. Having a child only fueled their cycle of violence.

Yet still, none of that could change how she felt. A life lived inside her. She could feel it with each step she took, and she felt stronger for it. She could feel it with each heartbeat, pulsing through her own.

Rea walked down the center of the village streets, heading back to her one-room cottage, feeling her world upside down, wondering what to think. *Pregnant*. She did not know how to be pregnant. She did not know how to give birth to a child, or how to raise one. She could barely feed herself. How would she even afford it?

Yet somehow she felt a new strength rising up within her. She felt it pumping in her veins, a strength she had only been dimly conscious of these last three moons, but which now came into crystal clear focus. It was a strength beyond hers. A strength of the future, of hope. Of possibility. Of a life she could never lead.

It was a strength that demanded her to be bigger than she could ever be.

As Rea walked slowly down the dirt street, she became dimly aware of her surroundings, and of the eyes of the villagers watching her. She turned, and on either side of the street saw the curious and disapproving eyes of old and young women, of old men and boys, of the lone survivors, maimed men who bore the scars of that night. They all held great suffering in their faces. And they all stared at her, at her stomach, as if she were somehow to blame.

She saw women her age amongst them, faces haunted, staring back with no compassion. Many of them, Rea knew, had been impregnated, too, and had already taken the root. She could see the grief in their eyes, and she could sense that they wanted her to share it.

Rea felt the crowd thicken around her and when she looked up she was surprised to see a wall of people blocking her path. The entire village seemed to have come out, men and women, old and young. She saw the agony in their faces, an agony she had shared, and she stopped and stared back at them. She knew what they wanted. They wanted to kill her boy.

She felt a sudden rush of defiance—and she resolved at that moment that she never would.

"Rea," came a tough voice.

Severn, a middle-aged man with dark hair and beard, and a scar across his cheek from that night, stood in their center and glared down at her. He looked her up and down as if she were a piece of cattle, and the thought crossed her mind that he was little better than the nobles. All of them were the same: all thought they had the right to control her body.

"You will take the root," he commanded darkly. "You will take the root, and tomorrow this shall all be behind you."

At Severn's side, a woman stepped forward. Luca. She had also been attacked that night, and had taken the root the week before.

Rea had heard her groaning all the night long, her wails of grief for her lost child.

Luca held out a sack, its yellow powder visible inside, and Rea recoiled. She felt the entire village looking to her, expecting her to reach out and take it.

"Luca will accompany you to the river," Severn added. "She will stay with you through the night."

Rea stared back, feeling a foreign energy rising within her as she looked at them all coldly.

She said nothing.

Their faces hardened.

"Do not defy us, girl," another man said, stepping forward, tightening his grip on his sickle until his knuckles turned white. "Do not dishonor the memory of the men and women we lost that night by giving life to their issue. Do what you are expected. Do what is your place."

Rea took a deep breath, and was surprised at the strength in her own voice as she answered:

"I will not."

Her voice sounded foreign to her, deeper and more mature than she had ever heard it. It was as if she had become a woman overnight.

Rea watched their faces flash with anger, like a storm cloud passing over a sunny day. One man, Kavo, frowned and stepped forward, an air of authority about him. She looked down and saw the flogger in his hand.

"There's an easy way to do this," he said, his voice full of steel. "And a hard way."

Rea felt her heart pounding as she stared back, looking him right in the eyes. She recalled what her father had told her once when she was a young girl: never back down. Not to anyone. Always stand up for yourself, even if the odds were against you. *Especially* if the odds were against you. Always set your sights on the biggest bully. Attack first. Even if it means your life.

Rea burst into action. Without thinking, she reached over, snatched a staff from one of the men's hands, stepped forward, and with all her might jabbed Kavo in the solar plexus.

Kavo gasped as he keeled over, and Rea, not giving him another chance, drew it back and jabbed him in the face. His nose cracked and he dropped the flogger and fell to the ground, clutching his nose and groaning into the mud.

Rea, still gripping the staff, looked up and saw the group of horrified, shocked faces staring back. They all looked a bit less certain.

"He is *my* boy," she spat. "I am keeping him. If you come for me, the next time it won't be a staff in your belly, but a sword."

With that, she tightened her grip on the staff, turned, and slowly walked away, elbowing her way through the crowd. Not one of them, she knew, would dare follow her. Not now, at least.

She walked away, her hands shaking, her heart pounding, knowing it would be a long six months until her baby came.

And knowing that the next time they came for her, they would come to kill.

CHAPTER THREE

Six Moons Later

Rea lay on the pile of furs beside her small, roaring fireplace, entirely and utterly alone, and groaned and shrieked in agony as her labor pains came. Outside, the winter wind howled as fierce gales slammed the shutters against the sides of the house and snow burst in drifts into the cottage. The raging storm matched her mood.

Rea's face was shiny with sweat as she sat beside the small fire, yet she could not get warm, despite the raging flames, despite the baby kicking and spinning in her stomach as if it were trying to leap out. She was wet and cold, shaking all over, and she felt certain that she would die on this night. Another labor pain came, and feeling the way she did, she wished the knight had just left her to be killed back then; it would have been more merciful. This slow, prolonged torture, this night of sheer agony, was a thousand times worse than anything he could have ever done to her.

Suddenly, rising even over her shrieks, over the gales of wind, there came another sound—perhaps the only sound left that was capable of sending a jolt of fear up her spine.

It was the sound of a mob. An angry mob of villagers, coming, she knew, to kill her child.

Rea summoned every last ounce of strength, strength she did not even know she had left, and, shaking, somehow managed to lift herself up off the floor. Groaning and screaming, she landed on her knees, wobbling. She reached out for a wooden peg on the wall, and with everything she had, with one great shriek she rose to standing.

She could not tell if it hurt more to be lying down or on her feet. But she had no time to ponder it. The mob grew louder, closer, and she knew they would soon arrive. Her dying would not bother her. But her baby dying—that was another matter. She had to get this child safe, no matter what it took. It was the strangest thing, but she felt more attached to the baby's life than her own.

Rea managed to stumble to the door and crashed into it, using the knob to hold herself up. She stood there, breathing hard for several seconds, resting on the knob, bracing herself. Finally, she turned it. She grabbed the pitchfork leaning against the wall and, propping herself up on it, opened the door.

Rea was met by a sudden gale of wind and snow, cold enough to take her breath away. The shouts met her, too, rising even over the wind, and her heart dropped to see in the distance the torches, winding their way toward her like enraged fireflies in the night. She glanced up at the sky and between the clouds caught a glimpse of a huge blood red moon, filling the sky. She gasped. It was not possible. She had never seen the moon shine red, and had never seen it in a storm. She felt a sharp kick in her stomach, and she suddenly knew, without a doubt, that that moon was a sign. It was meant for the birth of her child.

Who is he? she wondered.

Rea reached down and held her stomach with both hands as another person writhed inside her. She could feel his power, aching to break through, as if he were eager to fight this mob himself.

Then they came. The flaming torches lit the night as a mob appeared before her, emerging from the alleys, heading right for her. If she had been her old self, strong, able, she would have made a stand. But she could barely walk—barely stand—and she could not face them now. Not with her child about to come.

Even so, Rea felt a primal rage course through her, along with a primal strength, the primal strength, she knew, of her baby. She received a jolt of adrenaline, too, and her labor pains momentarily subsided. For a brief moment, she felt back to herself.

The first of the villagers arrived, a short, fat man, running for her, holding out a sickle. As he neared, Rea reached back, grabbed the pitchfork with both hands, stepped sideways, and released a primal scream as she drove it right through his gut.

The man stopped in shock, then collapsed at her feet. The mob stopped, too, looking at her in shock, clearly not expecting that.

Rea did not wait. She extracted the pitchfork in one quick motion, spun it overhead, and smashed the next villager across the cheek as he lunged at her with his club. He, too, dropped, landing in the snow at her feet.

Rea felt an awful pain in her side as another man rushed forward and tackled her, driving her down into the snow. They slid several feet, Rea groaning in pain as she felt the baby kicking within her. She wrestled with the man in the snow, fighting for her life, and as his grip momentarily loosened, Rea, desperate, sank her teeth into his cheek. He shrieked as she bit down hard, drawing blood, tasting it, not willing to let go, thinking of her baby.

Finally he rolled off of her, grabbing his cheek, and Rea saw her opportunity. Slipping in the snow, she crawled to her feet, ready to run. She was nearly there when suddenly she felt a hand grab her hair from behind. This man nearly yanked her hair out of her head as he pulled her back down to the ground and dragged her along. She looked back to see Severn scowling down at her.

"You should have listened when you had the chance," he seethed. "Now you will be killed, along with your baby."

Rea heard a cheer from the mob, and she knew she had reached her end. She closed her eyes and prayed. She had never been a religious person, but at this moment, she found God.

I pray, with every ounce of who I am, that this child be saved. You can let me die. Just save the child.

As if her prayers were answered, she suddenly felt the release of pressure on her hair, while at the same time she heard a thump. She looked up, startled, wondering what could have happened.

When she saw who had come to her rescue, she was stunned. It was a boy—Nick—several years younger than her. The son of a peasant farmer, like her, he had never been that bright, always picked on by the others. Yet she had always been kind to him. Perhaps he remembered.

She watched as Nick raised a club and smashed Severn in the side of the head, knocking him off of her.

Nick then faced off with the mob, holding out his club and blocking her from the others.

"Go quickly!" he yelled to her. "Before they kill you!"

Rea stared back at him with gratitude and shock. This mob would surely pummel him for what he'd done.

She jumped to her feet and ran, slipping as she went, determined to get far while she still had time. She ducked into alleyways, and before she disappeared, she glanced back to see Nick swinging wildly at the villagers, clubbing several of them. Several men, though, pressed forward and tackled him to the ground. With him out of the way, they ran after her.

Rea ran. Gasping for breath, she twisted and turned through the alleys, looking for shelter. Heaving, in horrific pain, she did not know how much farther she could go.

She finally found herself exiting into the village proper, with its elegant stone houses, and she glanced back with dread to see they were closing in, hardly twenty feet away. She gasped, stumbling more than running. She knew she was reaching her end. Another labor pain was coming.

Suddenly there came a sharp creak, and Rea looked up to see an ancient oak door before her open wide. She was startled to see Fioth, the old apothecary, peek out from his small stone fort, wide-eyed, beckoning her to enter quickly. Fioth reached out and yanked her with a grip surprisingly strong for his old age, and Rea found herself stumbling through the door of the luxurious keep.

He slammed and bolted it behind her.

A moment later the thumping came, the hands and sickles of dozens of irate villagers trying to knock it down. Yet the door held, to Rea's immense relief. It was a foot thick and centuries older than she. Its heavy iron bolts did not even bend.

Rea breathed deep. Her baby was safe.

Fioth leaned over and examined her, his face filled with compassion, and seeing his gentle look helped her more than anything else. No one had looked upon her with kindness in this village for months.

He removed her furs as she gasped from another labor pain. It was quiet in here, the gales of snow brushing the roof muted, and very warm.

Fioth led her to the fire's side and laid her down on a pile of furs. It was then that it all hit her: the running, the fighting, the pain. She collapsed. Even if there were a thousand men knocking down the door, she knew she could not move again.

She shrieked as a sharp labor pain tore through her.

"I can't run," Rea gasped, beginning to cry. "I cannot run anymore."

He ran a cool, damp cloth across her forehead.

"No need to run anymore," he said, his voice ancient, reassuring, as if he had seen it all before. "I am here now."

She shrieked and groaned as another pain ripped through her. She felt as if she were being torn in two.

"Lean back!" he commanded.

She did as she was told—and a second later, she felt it. A tremendous pressure between her legs.

There suddenly came a sound that terrified her.

A wail.

The scream of a baby.

She nearly blacked out from the pain.

She watched the apothecary's expert hands as she went in and out of consciousness, pulling the child from her, reaching out with something sharp, cutting the umbilical cord. She watched him wipe the baby with a cloth, clear its lungs, nose, throat.

The wail and scream came even louder.

Rea burst into tears. It was such a relief to hear the sound, penetrating her heart, rising even above the slamming of the villagers against the door. A child.

Her child.

He was alive. Against all odds, he had been born.

Rea was dimly aware of the apothecary wrapping him in a blanket, and then she felt the warmth as he placed him in her arms. She felt the weight of him on her chest, and she held him tight as he screamed and wailed. She had never been so overjoyed, tears gushing down her face.

Suddenly, there came a new sound: horses galloping. The clanging of armor. And then, shrieks. It was no longer the sound of the mob shouting to kill her—but rather, of the mob being killed itself.

Rea listened, baffled, trying to understand. Then she felt a wave of relief. Of course. The noble had come back to save her. To save his child.

"Thank God," she said. "The knights have come to my rescue."

Rea felt a sudden burst of optimism. Perhaps he would take her away from all this. Perhaps she would have a chance to start life over again. Her boy would grow up in a castle, become a great lord, and perhaps she would, too. Her baby would have a good life. *She* would have a good life.

Rea felt a flood of relief, tears of joy flooding her cheeks.

"No," the apothecary corrected, his voice heavy. "They have not come to save your baby."

She stared back, confused. "Then why have they come?"

He stared at her grimly.

"To kill it."

She stared back, aghast, feeling a cold dread run through her.

"They did not trust the job to a mob of villagers," he added. "They wanted to make sure it was done right, by their own hands."

Rea felt ice run through her veins.

"But…" she stammered, trying to understand, "…my baby belongs to the knight. Their commander. Why? Why would they want to kill it?"

Fioth shook his head grimly.

"Those men you hear are not his own. They are his rivals. They want his baby dead. They want *you* dead."

He stared back with a panicked urgency and she knew, with dread, that he spoke the truth.

"You must both flee this place!" he urged. "Now!"

He had hardly finished uttering the words when there came the crash of an iron pole against the door. This time it was no mere farmer's sickle—it was a professional knight's battering ram. As it hit, the door buckled.

Fioth turned to her, eyes wide in panic.

"GO!" he shouted.

Rea looked back at him, terror-stricken, wondering, in her condition, if she could even stand.

He grabbed her, though, and yanked her to her feet. She shrieked in pain, the motion pure agony.

"Please!" she cried. "It hurts too much! Let me die!"

"Look in your arms!" he cried back. "Do you want him to die?"

Rea looked down at the boy wailing in her arms, and as another smash came against the door, she knew he was right. She could not let him die here.

"What about you?" she moaned, realizing. "They will kill you, too."

He nodded with resignation.

"I have lived for many years," he replied. "If I can delay them from finding you, to give you a chance for safety, I will gladly give up what remains of my life. Now go! Head for the river! Find a boat and flee from here! Quickly!"

He yanked her before she had a chance to think, and before she knew it he was leading her to the rear entrance of his fort. He pulled back a tapestry to reveal a hidden door carved into the stone. He leaned against it with all his might and it opened with a scraping sound, releasing ancient air. A burst of cold air rushed into the fort.

Barely had it opened than he pushed her and her baby out the back.

Rea found herself immersed in the snowstorm, stumbling down a steep, snowy riverbank, clutching her baby. She slipped and slid, feeling as if the world were collapsing beneath her, barely able to move. As she ran, lightning struck an immense tree close to her, lighting up the night, and sent it crashing down too close to her, aflame.

Rea tumbled, and as she curled in with the urge to protect her baby, she felt the necklace that his father had given her for her baby come undone from around her neck, falling into the flames. Rea snapped off a thin twig to retrieve it, and succeeded in hooking it even as the twig caught light. She held it dangling for a moment, and was horrified to see her baby's hand reaching out for it.

The baby screamed, and Rea tossed the necklace aside, not caring now *who* had given it to her. She was horrified to see the perfect outline of the necklace on her baby's arm. It felt like an omen.

Rea slipped again as the terrain grew steep, and this time she landed on her butt. She went flying, and she cried out as the slope took her all the way down toward the riverbank.

She breathed with relief to reach it and realized if she hadn't slid all this way, she probably could not have made the run. She glanced back uphill, shocked at how far she had come, and watched in horror as the knights invaded Fioth's fort and set it ablaze. The fire burned strongly, even in the snow, and she felt an awful wave of guilt, knowing the old man had died for her.

A moment later knights burst out the back door, while more horses galloped around it. She could see they'd spotted her, and without pausing raced for her.

Rea turned and tried to run, but there was nowhere left to go. She was in no condition to run, anyway. All she could do was drop to her knees before the riverbank. She knew she would die here. She had reached the end of her rope.

Yet hope remained for her baby. She looked out and saw a tangle of sticks, perhaps a beaver's nest, so thick it resembled a basket. Driven by a mother's love, she thought quickly. She reached over and grabbed it and quickly placed her baby inside it. She tested it, and to her relief, it floated.

Rea reached out and prepared to shove the basket into the calm river's waters. If the current caught it, it would float away from here. Somewhere downriver. How far, and for how long, she did not know. But some chance of life was better than none.

Rea, weeping, leaned down and kissed her baby's forehead. She shrieked with grief, clasping her hands over both of his.

"I love you," she said, between sobs. "Never forget me."

The baby shrieked as if he understood, a piercing cry, rising even above the new clap of thunder and lightning, even above the sound of approaching horses.

Rea knew she could wait no longer. She gave the basket a push, and soon, the current caught it. She watched, sobbing, as it disappeared into the blackness.

She had no sooner lost sight of it than the clanging of armor appeared behind her—and she wheeled to find several knights dismounting, but feet away.

"Where's the child?" one demanded, his visor lowered, his voice cutting through the storm. It was nothing like the visor of the man who had had her. This man wore red armor, of a different shape, and there was no kindness in his voice.

"I…" she began.

Then she felt a fury within her—the fury of a woman who knew she was about to die. Who had nothing left to lose.

"He's gone," she spat, defiant. She smiled. "And you shall never have him. *Never.*"

The man groaned in anger as he stepped forward, drew a sword, and stabbed her.

Rea felt the awful agony of steel in her chest, and she gasped, breathless. She felt her world becoming lighter, felt herself immersed in white light, and she knew that this was death.

Yet, she felt no fear. Indeed, she felt satisfaction. Her baby was safe.

And as she landed face-first in the river, the waters turning red, she knew it was over. Her short, hard life had ended.

But her boy would live forever.

*

The peasant woman, Mithka, knelt by the river's edge, her husband beside her, the two frantically reciting their prayers, feeling no other recourse during this uncanny storm. It felt as if the end of the world were upon them. The blood red moon was a dire omen in and of itself—but appearing together with a storm like this, well, it was more than uncanny. It was unheard of. Something momentous, she knew, was afoot.

They knelt there together, gales of wind and snow whipping their faces, and she prayed for protection for their family. For mercy. For forgiveness for anything she may have done wrong.

A pious woman, Mithka had lived many sun cycles, had several children, had a good life. A poor life, but a good one. She was a decent woman. She had minded her business, had looked after others, and had never done harm to anyone. She prayed that God would protect her children, her household, whatever meager belongings they had. She leaned over and placed her palms in the snow, closed her eyes, and then bent low, touching her head to the ground. She prayed to God to show her a sign.

Slowly, she lifted her head. As she did, her eyes widened and her heart slammed at the sight before her.

"Murka!" she hissed.

Her husband turned and looked at it, too, and both knelt there, frozen, staring in astonishment.

It couldn't be possible. She blinked several times, and yet there it was. Before them, carried in the water's current, was a floating basket.

And in that basket was a baby.

A boy.

His screams pierced the night, rose even above the storm, above the impossible claps of thunder and lightning, and each scream pierced her heart.

She jumped into the river, wading in deep, ignoring the icy waters like knives on her skin, and grabbed the basket, fighting her way against the current and back toward shore. She looked down and saw the baby was meticulously wrapped in a blanket, and that he was, miraculously, dry.

She examined him more closely and was astonished to see the fresh burn on his arm—and even more astonished to see the outline of a symbol: two snakes circling a moon, a dagger between them.

She gasped; it was one she recognized immediately. A symbol she had heard of through folklore and legend. One she feared.

She turned to her husband.

"Who would do such a thing?" she asked, horrified, as she held him tight against her chest.

He could only shake his head in wonder.

"We must take him in," she decided.

Her husband frowned and shook his head.

"How?" he snapped. "We cannot afford to feed him. We can barely afford to feed us. We have three boys already—what do we need with a fourth? Our time raising children is done."

Mithka, thinking quick, showed him the burn on the baby's arm, knowing, after all these years, what would impress her husband. He clearly looked impressed.

"There," she snapped back. "There's a sign. A sign for us," she said sternly. "I am saving this baby—whether you like it or not. I will not leave him to die."

He still frowned, though less certain, as another lightning bolt struck above and he studied the skies with fear.

"And do you think it's a coincidence?" he asked. "A night like this, such a baby comes into this world? Have you any idea who you are holding?"

He looked down at the child with fear. And then he stood and backed away, finally turning and leaving, clearly displeased.

But Mithka would not give in. She smiled at the baby and rocked him to her chest, warming his cold face. Slowly, his crying calmed.

"A child unlike any of us," she replied to no one, holding him tight. "A child who shall change the world. And one I shall name: Royce."

PART TWO

CHAPTER FOUR

17 Sun Cycles later

Royce stood atop the hill, beneath the only oak tree in these fields of grain, an ancient thing whose limbs seemed to reach to the sky, and he looked deeply into Genevieve's eyes, deeply in love. They held hands as she smiled back at him, and as they leaned in and kissed, he felt in awe and gratitude that his heart could feel this full. As dawn broke over the fields of grain, Royce wished that he could freeze this moment forever.

Royce leaned back and looked at her. Genevieve was gorgeous. In her seventeenth year, as he was, she was tall, slim, with flowing blond hair and intelligent green eyes, a smattering of freckles across her dainty features. She had a smile that made him happy to be alive, and a laugh that put him at ease. More than that, she had a grace, a nobility, that far outmatched their peasant status.

Royce saw his own reflection in her eyes and he marveled that he looked as if he could be related to her. He was much bigger, of course, tall even for his age, with shoulders broader than even his older brothers', a strong chin, a noble nose, a proud forehead, an abundance of muscle which rippled beneath his frayed tunic, and light features, like hers. His longish blond hair fell just before his eyes, while his hazel-green eyes matched hers, albeit a shade darker. He'd been blessed with strength, and with a skill with the sword that matched his brothers', though he was the youngest of the four. His father had always joked that he had fallen from the sky, and Royce understood: he shared not his brothers' dark features or average frame. He was like a stranger in his own family.

They embraced, and it felt so good to be hugged so tightly, to have someone who loved him as much as he did her. The two of them had, in fact, been inseparable since they were children, had grown up together playing in these fields, had vowed even back then that on the summer solstice of their seventeenth year, they would wed. As children, it had been a deadly serious vow.

As they'd aged, year after year, they had not grown apart as most children do, but only closer together. Against all odds, their vow turned from a childish thing to something stronger, solemn,

22

unbreakable, year after year after year. Their lives, it seemed, were destined to never grow apart.

Now, finally, unbelievably, the day had arrived. Both were seventeen, the summer solstice had arrived, they were adults now, free to choose for themselves, and as they stood there, beneath that tree, watching the sun rise, they each knew, with giddy excitement, what that meant.

"Is your mother excited?" she asked.

Royce smiled.

"I think she loves you more than I, if that is possible," he laughed.

Genevieve's laugh reached his soul.

"And your parents?" he asked.

Her face darkened, just for a flash, and his heart fell.

"Is it me?" he asked.

She shook her head.

"They love you," she replied. "They just…" She sighed. "We are not wed yet. For them it could not come soon enough. They fear for me."

Royce understood. Her parents feared the nobles. Unwed peasants like Royce and Genevieve had no rights; if the nobles chose, they could come and take their women away, claim them for themselves. Until, that is, they were married. Then they would be safe.

"Soon enough," Genevieve said, her smile brightening.

"Are they relieved because it's me, or because, once wed, you'll be safe from the nobles?"

She laughed and mock hit him.

"They love you as the son they never had!" she said. "And I love you too. Here, take this."

She held out something tied on a string, little more than a tangled loop of wire, a lock of her hair inside. To Royce, though, it was more precious than anything he had seen. He took it and tucked it inside his shirt, close to his heart.

He caught her arms and kissed her.

"Royce!" cried a voice.

Royce turned to find his three brothers striding up the hill in a large group, Genevieve's sisters and cousins climbing up with them. They all held sickles and pitchforks, all of them ready for the day's labor, and Royce took a deep breath, knowing the time for parting had come. They were peasants, after all, and they could not afford to take an entire day off. The wedding would have to wait for sunset.

It did not bother Royce to work on this day, but he felt bad for Genevieve. He wished he could give her more.

"I wish you could take the day off," Royce said.

She smiled and then laughed.

"Working makes me happy. It takes my mind off things. Especially," she said, leaning in and kissing his nose, "of having to wait so long to see you again today."

They kissed, and she turned with a giggle and linked arms with her sisters and cousins and was soon bounding off to the fields with them, all of them giddy with happiness on this spectacular summer day.

Royce's brothers came up behind him, clasping his shoulders, and the four of them headed their own way, down the other side of the hill.

"Come on, loverboy!" Raymond said. The eldest son, he was like a father to Royce. "You can wait until tonight!"

His two other brothers laughed.

"She's really got him good," Lofen added, the middle of the bunch, shorter than the others but more stocky.

"There's no hope for you," Garet chimed in. The youngest of the three, just a few years older than Royce, he was closest to Royce, yet also felt their sibling rivalry the most. "Not even married yet, and already he's lost."

The three laughed, teasing him, and Royce smiled with them as they all headed off, as one, for the fields. He took one last glance over his shoulder and caught a glimpse of Genevieve disappearing down the hill. His heart lifted as she, too, looked back one last time and smiled at him from afar. The smile restored his soul.

Tonight, my love, he thought. *Tonight.*

*

Genevieve worked the fields, raising and swinging her sickle, surrounded by her sisters and cousins, a dozen of them, all laughing out loud on this auspicious day, as she worked halfheartedly. Genevieve stopped every few hacks to lean on the long shaft, look out at the blue skies and glorious yellow fields of wheat, and think of Royce. As she did, her heart beat faster. Today was the day she had always dreamt of, ever since she was a child. It was the most important day of her life. After today she and Royce would live together for the rest of their days; after this day, they would have their own cottage, a simple one-room dwelling on the edge of the fields, a humble place bequeathed to them by their parents. It would be a new beginning, a place to start life anew as husband and wife.

Genevieve beamed at the thought. There was nothing she had ever wanted more than to be with Royce. He had always been there, at her side, since she was a child, and she had never had eyes for anyone else. Though he was the youngest of his four brothers, she had always felt there was something special about Royce, something different about him. He was different from everyone around her, from anyone she had ever met. She did not know how, exactly, and she suspected that he did not either. But she saw something in him, something bigger than this village, this countryside. It was as if his destiny lay elsewhere.

"And what of his brothers?" asked a voice.

Genevieve snapped out of it. She turned to see Sheila, her eldest sister, giggling, two of her cousins behind her.

"After all, he has three! You can't have them all!" she added, laughing.

"Yes, what are you waiting for?" her cousin chimed in. "We've been waiting for an introduction."

Genevieve laughed.

"I *have* introduced you," she replied. "Many times."

"Not enough!" Sheila answered as the others laughed.

"After all, should not your sister marry his brother?"

Genevieve smiled.

"There is nothing I would like more," she replied. "But I cannot speak for them. I know only Royce's heart."

"Convince them!" her other cousin urged.

Genevieve laughed again. "I shall do my best."

"And what will you wear?" her cousin interjected. "You still haven't decided which dress you shall—"

A noise suddenly cut through the air, one which immediately filled Genevieve with a sense of dread, made her let go of her sickle and turn to the horizon. She knew before she even fully heard it that it was an ominous noise, the sound of trouble.

She turned and studied the horizon and as she did, her worst fears were confirmed. The sound of galloping became audible, and over the hill, there appeared an entourage of horses. Her heart lurched as she noticed their riders were clothed in the finest silks, as she saw their banner, the green and the gold, a bear in the center, heralding the house of Nors.

The nobles were coming.

Genevieve flushed with ire at the sight. These greedy men had tithe after tithe from her family, from all the peasants' families.

They sucked everyone dry while they lived like kings. And yet still, it was not enough.

Genevieve watched them ride, and she prayed with all she had that they were just riding by, that they would not turn her way. After all, she had not seen them in these fields for many sun cycles.

Yet Genevieve watched with despair as they suddenly turned and rode right for her.

No, she willed silently. *Not now. Not here. Not today.*

Yet they rode and rode, getting closer and closer, clearly coming for her. Word must have spread of her wedding day, and that always made them eager to take what they could, before it was too late.

The other girls gathered around her instinctively, coming close. Sheila turned to her and clutched her arm frantically.

"RUN!" she commanded, shoving her.

Genevieve turned and saw open fields before her for miles. She knew how foolish it would be—she would not get far. She would still be taken—but without dignity.

"No," she replied, cool, calm.

Instead, she tightened her grip on her sickle and held it before her.

"I shall face them head-on."

They looked back at her, clearly stunned.

"With your sickle?" her cousin asked doubtfully.

"Perhaps they do not come in malice," her other cousin chimed in.

But Genevieve watched them come, and slowly, she shook her head.

"They do," she replied.

She watched them near and expected them to slow—yet to her surprise, they did not. In their center rode Manfor, a privileged noble in his twentieth year, whom she despised, the duke of the kingdom, a boy with wide lips, light eyes, golden locks, and a permanent sneer. He appeared as if he were constantly looking down on the world.

As he neared, Genevieve saw he wore a cruel smile on his face, as he looked over her body as if it were a piece of meat. Hardly twenty yards away, Genevieve raised her sickle and stepped forward.

"They shall not take me," she said, resigned, thinking of Royce. She wished more than anything that he was at her side right now.

"Genevieve, don't!" Sheila cried.

Genevieve ran toward them with the sickle high, feeling the adrenaline course through her. She did not know how she summoned the courage, but she did. She charged forward, raised the sickle, and slashed it down at the first noble that came for her.

But they were too fast. They rode in like thunder, and as she swung, one merely raised his club, swung it around, and smashed the sickle from her hand. She felt an awful vibration through her hands and watched, hopeless, as her weapon went flying, landing in the stalks nearby.

A moment later, Manfor galloped past, leaned down, and backhanded her across the face with his metal gauntlet.

Genevieve cried out, spun around from the force of it, and landed face first in the stalks, stung by the searing pain.

The horses came to an abrupt stop, and as the riders dismounted all around her, Genevieve felt rough hands on her. She was yanked to her feet, delirious from the blow.

She stood there, wobbly, and looked up to see Manfor standing before her. He sneered down as he raised his helmet and removed it.

"Let go of me!" she hissed. "I am not your property!"

She heard cries and looked over to see her sisters and cousins rushing forward, trying to save her—and she watched in horror as the knights backhanded each one, sending them to the ground.

Genevieve heard Manfor's awful laughter as he grabbed her and threw her on the back of his horse, binding her wrists together. A moment later he mounted behind her, kicked, and rode off, the girls shrieking behind her as she rode further and further away. She tried to struggle but was helpless to fight back as he held her in a vise-like grip.

"How wrong you are, young girl," he replied, laughing as he rode. "You are mine."

CHAPTER FIVE

Royce stood amidst the wheat fields, hacking away with his sickle, his heart filled with joy as he thought of his bride. He could hardly believe his wedding day had arrived. He had loved Genevieve for as long as he could remember, and this day would be a day to rival no others. Tomorrow, he would wake with her by his side, in a new cottage of their own, with a new life ahead of them. He could feel the flurries in his stomach. There was nothing he wished for more.

As he swung the sickle, Royce thought of his nightly training with his brothers, the four of them sparring incessantly with wooden swords, and sometimes with real ones, double-weighted, nearly impossible to lift, to make them stronger, faster. Although he was younger than his three brothers, Royce realized he was already a better fighter than them all, more agile with the sword, faster to strike and to defend. It was as if he were cut from a different cloth. He was different, he knew that. Yet he did not know how. And that troubled him.

Where, he wondered, had his fighting talents come from? Why was he so different? It made little sense. They were all brothers, all of the same blood, the same family. Yet at the same time the four of them were inseparable, doing everything together, whether it was sparring or working the fields. That, in fact, was his one touch of apprehension to this joyful day: would his moving out be the beginning of their growing apart? He vowed silently that, no matter what, he would not allow it to be.

Royce's thoughts were suddenly interrupted by a sound at the edge of the field, an unusual sound for this time of day, a sound he did not want to hear on a perfect day like this. Horses. Galloping with urgency.

Royce turned and looked, instantly alarmed, and his brothers did, too. His alarm only deepened as he spotted Genevieve's sisters and cousins riding for him. Even from here Royce could see their faces etched with panic, with urgency.

Royce struggled to comprehend what he was seeing. Where was Genevieve? Why were they all riding for him?

And then his heart sank as he realized that clearly something terrible had happened.

He dropped his sickle, as did his brothers and the dozen other peasant farmers of their village, and ran out to meet them. The first to meet him was Sheila, Genevieve's sister, and she dismounted before her horse had come to a stop, clutching Royce's shoulders.

"What is it?" Royce called out. He grabbed her shoulders, and he could feel her shaking.

She could barely get the words out between her tears.

"Genevieve!" she cried out, terror in her voice. "They've taken her!"

Royce felt his stomach plummet at her words, as worst-case scenarios rushed into his mind.

"Who?" he demanded, as his brothers ran up beside him.

"Manfor!" she cried. "Of the House of Nors!"

Royce felt his heart slamming in his chest, as waves of indignation coursed through him. His bride. Snatched away by the nobles, as if she were their property. His face burned red.

"When!?" he demanded, squeezing Sheila's arm harder than he meant to.

"Just now!" she replied. "We got these horses to come tell you as soon as we could!"

The others dismounted behind her, and as they did they all handed the reins to Royce and his brothers. Royce did not hesitate. In one quick motion he mounted her horse, kicked, and was tearing through the fields.

Behind him, he could hear his brothers riding, too, none missing a beat, all heading through the stalks and for the distant fort.

His eldest brother, Raymond, rode up beside him.

"You know the law is on his side," he called out. "He is a noble, and she is unwed—at least for now."

Royce nodded back.

"If we storm the fort and ask for her back, they will refuse," Raymond added. "We have no legal grounds to demand her back."

Royce gritted his teeth.

"I'm not going to ask for her back," he replied. "I'm going to take her back."

Lofen shook his head as he rode up beside them.

"You'll never make it through those doors," he called out. "A professional army awaits you. Knights. Armor. Weaponry. Gates." He shook his head again. "And even if you somehow manage to get past them, even if you manage to rescue her, they will not let her go. They will hunt you down and kill you."

"I know," Royce called back.

"My brother," Garet called out. "I love you. And I love Genevieve. But this will mean the death of you. The death of us all. Let her go. There is nothing you can do."

Royce could hear how much his brothers cared for him, and he appreciated it—but he could not allow himself to listen. That was *his* bride, and whatever the stakes, he had no choice. He could not abandon her, even if it meant his death. It was who he was.

Royce kicked his horse harder, not wanting to hear any more, and galloped faster through the fields, toward the horizon, toward the sprawling town where Manfor's fort stood. Toward what would surely be his death.

Genevieve, Royce thought. *I'm coming for you.*

*

Royce rode with all he had across the fields, his three brothers at his side, cresting the final hill and then charging down for the sprawling town that lay below. In its center sat a massive fort, the home of the House of Nors, the nobles who ruled his land with an iron fist, who had bled his family dry, demanding tithe after tithe of everything they farmed. They had managed to keep the peasants poor for generations. They had dozens of knights at their disposal, in full armor, with real weapons and real horses; they had thick stone walls, a moat, a bridge, and they kept watch over the town like a jealous hen, under the pretense of keeping law and order—but really just to milk it dry.

They made the law. They enforced the cruel laws that were passed down by all the nobles throughout the land, laws that only benefited *them*. They operated in the guise of offering protection, yet all the peasants knew that the only protection they needed was from the nobles themselves. The kingdom of Sevania, after all, was a safe kingdom, isolated from other lands by water on three sides, at the northern tip of the Alufen continent. A strong ocean, rivers, and mountains offered thick walls of security. The land had not been invaded in centuries.

The only danger and tyranny lay from within, from the noble aristocracy and what they milked from the poor. People like Royce. Now even riches were not enough—they had to have their wives, too.

The thought brought color to Royce's cheeks. He lowered his head and braced himself as he tightened his grip on his sword.

"The bridge is down!" Raymond called out. "The portcullis is open!"

Royce noticed it himself and took it as an encouraging sign.

"Of course it is!" Lofen called back. "Do you really think they are expecting an attack? Least of all from us?"

Royce rode faster, grateful for his brothers' companionship, knowing all his brothers felt as strongly for Genevieve as he did. She was like a sister to them, and an affront to Royce was an affront to them all. He looked out ahead and on the drawbridge spotted a few of the castle's knights, halfheartedly looking at the pastures and fields surrounding the town. They were unprepared. They had not been attacked in centuries and had no reason to expect to be now.

Royce drew his sword with a distinctive ring, lowered his head, and held the sword high. The sound of swords rang through the air as his brothers drew, too. Royce kicked out front to take the lead, wanting to be the first into battle. His heart pounded with excitement and fear—not fear for himself, but for Genevieve.

"I will get in and find her and get out!" Royce called out to his brothers, formulating a plan. "You all stay outside the perimeter. This is my fight."

"We shall not let you go inside alone!" Garet called back.

Royce shook his head, adamant.

"If something goes wrong, I don't want you paying the price," he called back. "Stay out here and distract those guards. That is what I need the most."

He pointed with his sword at a dozen knights standing at the gatehouse beside the moat. Royce knew that as soon as he rode over the bridge they would break into action; but if his brothers distracted them, it could perhaps keep them at bay just long enough for Royce to get inside and find her. All he needed, he figured, was a few minutes. If he could find her quickly, he could snatch her and ride away and be free of this place. He did not want to kill anyone if he could help it; he did not even want to harm them. He just wanted his bride back.

Royce lowered his head and galloped as fast as he possibly could, so fast he could hardly breathe, the wind whipping his hair and face. He closed in on the bridge, thirty yards away, twenty, ten, the sound of his horse and his heartbeat thundering in his ears. His heart slammed in his chest as he rode, realizing how insane this was. He was about to do what the peasant class would never dream of doing: attack the gentry. It was a war he could not possibly win, and a sure way to get killed. And yet his bride lay behind those gates, and that was enough for him.

Royce was so close now, but a few yards away from reaching the bridge, and he looked up and saw the knights' eyes widen in surprise as they fumbled with their weapons, caught off guard, clearly not expecting anything like this.

Their delayed reaction was just what Royce needed. He raced forward and, as they raised their halberds, he lowered his sword and, aiming for the shafts, cut them in half. He slashed from side to side, destroying the weapons of the knights on either side of the bridge, careful not to harm them if he didn't need to. He just wanted to disarm them, and not get bogged down in combat.

Royce gained speed, urging his horse on, and he rode even faster, using his horse as a weapon, bumping the remaining guards hard enough to send them flying, in their heavy armor, over the sides of the narrow bridge, and into the moat's waters below. It would take them a long while, Royce realized, to get out. And that was all the time he needed.

Behind him, Royce could hear his brothers helping his cause; on the far side of the bridge they rode for the gatehouse, slashing at the guards, disarming them before they had a chance to rally. They managed to block and bar the gatehouse, keeping the flummoxed knights off guard, and giving Royce the cover he needed.

Royce lowered his head and charged for the open portcullis, riding faster as he watched it begin to lower. He lowered his head and managed to burst through the open arch right before the heavy portcullis closed for good.

Royce rode into the inner courtyard, heart pounding, and took stock, looking all around. He'd never been inside and was disoriented, finding himself surrounded by thick stone walls on all sides, several stories high. Servants and common folk bustled to and fro, carrying buckets of water and other wares. Luckily, no knights awaited him inside. Of course, they had no cause to expect an attack.

Royce scanned the walls, desperate for any sign of his bride.

Yet he found none. He received a jolt of panic. What if they had taken her elsewhere?

"GENEVIEVE!" he called out.

Royce looked everywhere, frantically turning on his neighing horse. He had no idea where to look, and had no plan. He had not even thought he would make it this far.

Royce racked his brain, needing to think quick. The nobles likely lived upstairs, he figured, away from the stench, the masses, where the wind and sunlight was strong. Naturally, that was where they would take Genevieve.

The thought inflamed him with rage.

Forcing his emotions in check, Royce kicked his horse and galloped across the courtyard, past shocked servants who stopped and stared, dropping their work as he raced by. He spotted a wide, spiral stone staircase across the way and he rode all the way to it, dismounting before the horse could even stop, hitting the ground at a run and sprinting up the stairs. He ran around and around the spirals, again and again, ascending flight after flight. He had no idea where he was going, but figured he would start at the top.

Royce finally exited the staircase at the highest landing, breathing hard.

"Genevieve!" he cried out, hoping, praying for a response.

There was none. His dread deepened.

He chose a corridor and ran down it, praying it was the right one. As he raced past, a man suddenly burst open a door and stuck his head out. It was a noble, a short, fat man with a broad nose and thinning hair.

He scowled at Royce, clearly summing him up from his garb as a peasant; he wrinkled his nose as if something unpleasant had entered his midst.

"Hey!" he shouted. "What are you doing in our—"

Royce did not hesitate. As the indignant noble lunged for him, he punched him in the face, knocking him flat on his back.

Royce checked quickly inside the open door, hoping for a glimpse of her. But it was empty.

He continued to run.

"GENEVIEVE!" Royce cried.

Suddenly, he heard a cry, far away, in response.

His heart stopped as he stood still and listened, wondering where it had come from. Aware that his time was limited, that an entire army would soon be chasing after him, he continued running, heart pounding, calling her name again and again.

Again there came a muffled cry, and Royce knew it was her. His heart slammed. She was up here. And he was getting closer.

Royce finally reached the end of the corridor and as he did, from behind the last door on the left, he heard a cry. He did not hesitate as he lowered his shoulder and smashed open the ancient oak door.

The door shattered and Royce stumbled inside and found himself standing in an opulent chamber, thirty by thirty feet, with soaring ceilings, windows carved into the stone walls, a massive fireplace, and, in the center of the room, a huge, luxurious four-poster bed, unlike anything Royce had ever seen. He felt a surge of relief as he saw there, in a pile of furs, his love, Genevieve.

33

She was, he was relieved to see, fully clothed, still flailing, kicking, as Manfor tried to wrestle her from behind. Royce fumed. There he was, clawing at his bride, trying to strip her clothes. Royce was elated that he'd made it in time.

Genevieve writhed, trying valiantly to get him off her, but Manfor was too strong for her.

Without a moment's hesitation, Royce burst into action. He rushed forward and pounced, just as Manfor spun to look. As his eyes widened in shock, Royce grabbed him by the shirt and threw him.

Manfor went flying across the room and landed hard on the cobblestone, groaning.

"Royce!" Genevieve called out, her voice filled with relief as she spun and faced him.

Royce knew he could not give Manfor a chance to recover. As he tried to rise, Royce jumped on top of him, pinning him down. Flooded with rage for what he had done to his wife, Royce pulled back his fist and punched him once, hard in the jaw.

Manfor bounced back, though, sitting up and reaching for a dagger. But Royce snatched it from his hand and pounded him again and again. Manfor fell back, and Royce knocked the dagger away, sliding it across the floor.

He held Manfor in a lock and Manfor sneered back, ever defiant and superior.

"The law is on my side," Manfor seethed. "I can take anyone I want. She is mine."

Royce scowled.

"You cannot take my bride."

"You're mad," Manfor countered. "*Mad*. You will be killed by the end of the day. There's nowhere to hide. Don't you know that? We own this country."

Royce shook his head.

"What you don't understand," he said, "is that I don't care."

Manfor frowned.

"You won't get away with this," Manfor said. "I will see to it."

Royce tightened his grip on Manfor's wrists.

"You will do nothing of the sort. Genevieve and I will leave here today. If you come after her again, I will kill you."

To Royce's surprise, Manfor smiled an evil smile, blood trickling from his mouth.

"I will *never* let her be," Manfor replied. "*Ever*. I will torment her the rest of her life. And I will hunt you down like a dog with all my father's men. I will take her, and she will be mine. And you will

34

be hanged on the gallows. So run now and remember her face—for soon enough, she will be mine."

Royce felt a hot flush of rage. What was worse than these cruel words was that he knew them to be true. There was nowhere to run; the nobles owned the countryside. He could not fight an army. And Manfor, indeed, would never give up. For cruel sport—for no other reason. He had so much, and yet he could not help but deprive people who had nothing.

Royce looked down into this cruel noble's eyes and he knew that Genevieve would be had by this man one day. And he knew he could not allow it to happen. He wanted to walk away, he really did. But he could not. To do so would mean Genevieve's death.

Royce suddenly grabbed Manfor and threw him to his feet. He faced him and drew his sword.

"Draw!" Royce commanded, giving him a chance to fight honorably.

Manfor stared back, clearly surprised that he would be given this chance. Then he drew his sword.

Manfor charged, swinging down hard, and Royce raised his sword and blocked it, sparks flying. Royce, sensing he was stronger, raised his sword, pushing Manfor back, then spun with his elbow and smashed him in the face with the hilt.

There came a crack as Royce broke Manfor's nose. Manfor stumbled back and stared, clearly stunned as he grabbed at his nose. Royce could have taken the moment to kill him, but again, he gave him another chance.

"Back down now," Royce offered, "and I shall let you live."

Manfor, though, let out a groan of fury. He raised his sword and charged again.

Royce blocked, while Manfor swung furiously, each slashing back and forth, swords clanging as sparks flew, driving each other back and forth across the room. Manfor might be a noble, raised with all the benefits of the royal class, yet still Royce had superior fighting talent.

As they fought, Royce's heart sank as he heard distant horns, heard the sound of an army closing in on the castle, the horses' hooves clomping on the cobblestone below. He knew his time was running out. Something had to be done fast.

Finally Royce spun Manfor's sword around sharply and disarmed him, sending it flying through the air and across the room. Royce held his tip to Manfor's throat.

"Back away, now," Royce commanded.

Manfor slowly backed away, arms up. Yet when he reached a small wooden desk, he suddenly spun, grabbed something, and threw it at Royce's eyes.

Royce shrieked as he was suddenly blinded. His eyes stung as his world turned black and he realized, too late, as he groped at his eyes, what it was: ink. It was a dirty move, a move unbecoming a noble, or any fighter. But then again, Royce knew he should not be surprised.

Before he could regain his sight, Royce suddenly felt a sharp blow to his stomach as he was kicked. He keeled over, dropping to the floor, winded, and as he looked up, he regained just enough of his vision to watch Manfor smile as he extracted a hidden dagger from his cloak—and raised it for Royce's back.

"ROYCE!" Genevieve screamed out.

As the dagger plunged down for his back, Royce managed to collect himself, rising to one knee, raising his arm, and grabbing Manfor's wrist. Royce slowly stood, arms shaking, and as Manfor continued to lower the dagger, he suddenly sidestepped and spun Manfor's arm around, using his force against him. Manfor kept swinging, though, unwilling to stop, and this time, as Royce stepped aside, he plunged the dagger into his own stomach.

Manfor gasped. He stood there, staring back, eyes wide, blood trickling from his mouth. He was dying.

Royce felt the solemnity of the moment. He had killed a man. For the first time in his life, he had killed a man. And no ordinary man—but a noble.

Manfor's last gesture was a cruel smile, blood pouring from his mouth.

"You have won back your bride," he gasped, "at the cost of your life. You'll be joining me soon enough."

With that, Manfor collapsed and landed on the floor with a thump.

Dead.

Royce turned to look at Genevieve, who sat on the bed, stunned. He could see the relief and gratitude on her face. She jumped up from the bed, ran across the room, and into his arms. He embraced her tightly, and it felt so good. All made sense in the world again.

"Oh, Royce," she said in his ear, and that was all she needed to say. He understood.

"Come, we must go," Royce said. "Our time is short."

He took her hand and the two of them burst out the open door of the chamber and into the corridors.

Royce ran down the hall, Genevieve beside him, his heart pounding as he heard the royal horns being sounded, again and again. He knew it was the sound of alarm—and he knew it was meant for him.

Hearing the clanging of armor down below, Royce knew the fort was sealed off, and that he was surrounded. His brothers had done a good job of holding them off, but Royce's raid had taken too long. As they ran he glanced down into the courtyard, and his heart dropped to see dozens of knights already pouring through the gates.

Royce knew there was no way out. Not only had he broken into their home, he had killed one of their own, a noble, a member of the royal family. They would not, he knew, let him live. Today would be the day his life changed forever. How ironic, he thought; this morning he had awakened so filled with joy, so anticipating the day. Now, before the sun had set on that same day, he would instead likely be facing the gallows.

Royce and Genevieve ran and ran, nearing the end of the hall and the entrance to the spiral staircase—when suddenly a half dozen knights appeared, emerging from the steps, blocking their way.

Royce and Genevieve stopped short, turned, and ran the other way, as the knights pursued them. Royce could hear their armor clanging behind him, and he knew his only advantage was his lack of armor, giving him just enough speed to keep ahead of them.

They ran and ran, twisting down corridors, Royce desperately hoping to find a rear staircase, another way out—when suddenly they turned down another corridor and found themselves facing a stone wall. Royce's heart dropped as they slammed to a stop.

A dead end.

Royce spun and drew his sword while putting Genevieve behind him, prepared to make a stand against the knights even though he knew it would be his last.

Suddenly he felt Genevieve clutch his arm frantically as she cried: "Royce!"

He spun and saw what she was looking at: a large, open-air window beside them. He looked down and his stomach sank. It was a long drop, way too long to survive.

And yet he saw her pointing to a wagon full of hay ambling by beneath them.

"We can jump!" she cried.

She took his hand, and together, they stepped up toward the window. He turned and looked back, saw the knights closing in, and suddenly, before he had time to think through how crazy this was, he felt his hand yanked—and they were airborne.

Genevieve was even braver than he. She always had been, even as kids, he recalled.

They jumped, falling a good thirty feet through the air, Royce's stomach in his throat, Genevieve shrieking, as they aimed for the wagon. Royce braced himself to die, and was grateful that he would not die, at least, at the hands of the nobles—and with his love at his side.

To Royce's immense relief they landed in the pile of hay. It shot up in a huge cloud around them as they did, and while he was winded and bruised from the fall, to his amazement, he did not break anything. He sat up immediately and looked over to see if Genevieve was okay; she lay there in a daze, but she, too, sat up, and as she brushed off the hay, he saw with immense relief that she was unhurt.

Without a word they both at the same time remembered their predicament and jumped from the cart, Royce taking her hand. Royce ran to his horse, still awaiting him in the courtyard, mounted it, grabbed Genevieve, and helped her up behind him. With a kick the two of them took off at a gallop, Royce aiming for the open gate to the castle, as knights continued to flood in, racing past them, not even realizing it was them.

They neared the open gate and Royce's heart pounded in his chest; they were so close. All they had to do was clear it, and with a few strides they would be out in the open countryside. From there they could rally with his brothers, his cousins, and men, and together, they could all flee from this place, and start life anew somewhere. Or better yet, they could amass their own army and fight these nobles once and for all. For one glorious moment time stood still, as Royce felt himself on the precipice of change, of victory, of everything he had known being turned upside down. The day for revolt had come. The day for their lives to never be the same again.

As Royce neared the gate, his veins filled with cold dread as he watched the portcullis, open again to let knights in, suddenly lowered, slamming shut before him. His horse reared, and they stopped short.

Royce turned around, looking back into the courtyard. There he saw fifty knights, now realizing who they were, closing in. Royce prepared to ride forward, to meet them in battle, however foolhardy it was, when suddenly, he felt a rope landing on him from behind, and heard Genevieve cry out.

The ropes tightened around his waist, and with a jerk, Royce felt himself thrown backward from his horse. He landed on the ground hard, winded, bound from behind. He looked over and saw Genevieve bound by ropes, too, also yanked to the ground.

Royce rolled and stumbled, frantically trying to break free, the ropes tight around his arms and shoulders. He reached down to his waist, grabbed his dagger, and with one jerk, managed to cut them loose.

Free, he rolled out of the way of a club as it came down for his head. He reached out and grabbed his attacker's sword, and then he wheeled, standing in the center of the courtyard, surrounded by what was now nearly a hundred knights. They closed in on him from all sides.

They charged. Royce raised his sword and fought back, defending as they slashed, slashing back himself, feeling invincible, stronger and faster than all of them. Still, they closed in tighter and tighter, their ranks growing thicker.

Royce raised his sword and blocked a blow aimed for his head; he then spun and slashed at another sword aiming for his back, and slashed up and knocked the sword from his attacker's hands. He leaned back and kicked another knight in the chest as he neared, forcing him to drop his club.

Royce fought like a man possessed, slashing and parrying, managing to keep dozens of them at bay, as swords clanged and sparks showered down all around him. He breathed hard, barely able to see from the sweat stinging his eyes. And all the while he thought of only one thing: Genevieve. He would die here for her.

The ranks thickened even more, and soon, it was too much even for him. Royce's arms and shoulders ached, his breathing grew heavy, as he found the crowd so thick, so close, that he could barely maneuver to swing. He raised his sword one last time to slash, when suddenly, he felt an awful pain in the back of his head.

He dropped to the ground, dimly aware he had been clubbed. The next thing he knew he was lying sideways on the ground, unable to move, as dozens of knights pounced on him. It was a wall of metal pinning him to the ground, bending his arms, knees in his back, arms on his head.

It was over, he realized.

He had lost.

CHAPTER SIX

Royce woke, startled, to the feeling of ice water on his face, to the sounds of shouts and jeers, and he squinted in the light. One of his eyes, he realized right away, was sealed shut, the other barely open, just enough for him to see by. His head reeled from the pain, his body stiff, covered in lumps and bruises, and he felt as if he had been rolled down a mountain. He looked out at the world before him, and wished he hadn't.

A bustling mob encircled him, some shouting and jeering, others protesting, seemingly on his behalf. It was as though these people had erupted in civil war, he in the center. He struggled to make sense of what he saw. Was this, he wondered, a dream?

The pain was too intense for this to be a dream; the stabbing headache, the coarse ropes digging into his wrists. He struggled, to no avail, at the ropes binding his wrists and ankles and looked down to realize he was tied to a stake. His heart pounded to see a pile of wood beneath him, as if ready to be lit. Fear crept over him as he realized he was strung up in the castle courtyard.

Royce looked out and saw hundreds of villagers swarming into the courtyard, saw dozens of knights and guards standing along the walls; he saw a makeshift wooden stage, perhaps fifty feet away, and on it, tribunal judges, all nobles. In the center sat a man he recognized: Lord Nors. The head of the nobles' family. Manfor's father. He was the presiding judge of the countryside. And he sat in the center and stared down at Royce with a hatred unlike any Royce had seen.

It did not bode well.

All of it came rushing back to Royce. Genevieve. Breaking into the fort. Rescuing her. Killing Manfor. Jumping. Fighting off those knights. And then...

There came the slamming of a hammer on wood several times, and the crowd quieted. Lord Nors stood, glowering down at all, and he was even more fierce, more commanding, standing. He set his fury-filled eyes on Royce and Royce realized he was being put on trial. He had seen several trials before, and none had gone well for the prisoners.

Royce scanned the faces, desperate to find any glimpse of Genevieve, praying she was safe, away from all this.

Yet he found none. That was what worried him most of all. Had she been imprisoned? Killed?

He tried to block out various nightmare scenarios from his mind.

"You hereby stand accused of the murder of Manfor of the House of Nors, son of Lord Nors, ruler of the South and the Woods of Segall," Lord Nors boomed out, and the crowd grew completely still. "What is your plea?"

Royce opened his mouth, struggled to speak—but his lips and throat were parched. His voice fell short, and he tried again.

"He stole my bride," Royce finally managed to reply.

There came a chorus of supportive cheers, and Royce looked out to see thousands of villagers, his countrymen, pouring in, wielding clubs and sickles and pitchforks. His heart leapt with hope and gratitude as he realized all his people had come to support him. They had all had enough.

Royce looked up at Lord Nors and saw him lose his conviction, just a touch. A nervous look spread across his face as he turned and looked to his fellow judges and they looked to the knights. It seemed as if they were beginning to realize that they might, if they condemned Royce to death, have a revolution on their hands.

Finally, Lord Nors slammed his hammer, and the crowd quieted.

"And yet," he boomed, "the law is clear: any peasant woman is the property of any noble until she is wed."

There came a loud chorus of boos and hisses from the crowd, and the mob surged forward. An anonymous person hurled a tomato toward the stage, and the crowd cheered, as it barely missed Lord Nors.

There came a horrified gasp amongst the nobles, and as Lord Nors nodded, the knights began to push into the crowd, eager to find the offender. Yet they soon stopped and thought better of it as they were swarmed by hundreds more villagers bustling into the square, making passage impossible. One knight attempted to elbow his way forward, but he soon found himself completely engulfed by the masses, shoved every which way, and amidst angry shouts and cheers, he backed away.

The crowd cheered. Finally, they were standing up for themselves.

Royce felt a surge of optimism. A turning point had arrived. All the peasants, like he, had had enough. No one wanted their women taken anymore. No one wanted to be thought of as property. All of them realized that they could be in Royce's position.

Royce scanned the mob, still desperate to find Genevieve—and his heart suddenly leapt as he spotted her at the edge of the courtyard, bound in ropes. Nearby stood his three brothers; they, too, were bound. He was relieved to see that at least they were alive, and uninjured. But upset to see them bound. He wondered what would become of them, and he wished more than anything that he could take their punishment for them.

As the crowd swelled, the magistrates looked more nervous than before, and they looked to Lord Nors with uncertain glances.

"It is *your* law!" Royce called out, finding his voice, emboldened. "Not ours!"

The crowd let out an enormous roar of approval, as it surged forward dangerously, pitchforks and sickles raised high in the air.

Lord Nors, scowling back down at Royce, held up his hands, and the crowd finally quieted.

"My son is dead on this day," he boomed, his voice heavy with grief. "And if I were to uphold the law, you would be killed, too."

The crowd booed and swarmed threateningly.

"And yet," Lord Nors boomed, raising his hands, "given the situation of our times, killing you would not be in the best interests of the crown. And thus," he said, turning and looking to his fellow magistrates, "I have decided to grant you mercy!"

There came a great cheer from the crowd, rippling through in waves, and Royce felt a surge of relief. Lord Nors raised his hands.

"Your brothers killed none of our men in your raid, and thus they shall not be killed, either."

The crowd cheered.

"They shall be imprisoned!" he boomed.

The crowd booed.

"Yet your bride-to-be," Lord Nors boomed, "shall never be yours. She shall become the property of one of our nobles."

The crowd booed and hissed, but before they could get any louder, Lord Nors finished, pointing down at Royce with all his wrath:

"And you, Royce, shall be sentenced to the Pits!"

The crowd booed and rushed forward, and soon a brawl erupted in the streets.

Royce did not have a chance to watch it unfold. Suddenly the ropes were severed from his wrists and ankles, and he fell to the ground, limp. He felt arms all around him, metal gauntlets grabbing him, dragging him away through the chaos.

As he was dragged through the crowd, Lord Nors's words echoed in his mind. *The Pits.* Royce felt a deepening sense of foreboding. It was the brutal bloodsport for the nobles' entertainment, one no one survived. Lord Nors had shrewdly spared him a death sentence to appease the masses—and yet the Pits were a sentence worse than death. It was a crafty move. Lord Nors had spared a revolution, and yet had still managed to kill Royce.

Royce was crestfallen. Better to have died here, nobly, before his people, than to be shipped off to die an even more horrible death.

Yet as he was dragged through the rioting crowd, toward the towering arches to the city's exit, Royce thought not of himself but of Genevieve. She was all that mattered to him now. She was all that had ever mattered to him. The idea of her being given to another noble was too much for him. It made all of this futile.

Royce bucked and writhed, trying uselessly to get free. He glanced back as they dragged him, hoping for one last glimpse of her.

"Genevieve!" he called.

He spotted a glimpse of her between the swarming crowd.

"Royce!" she called back, weeping.

Yet there was nothing either of them could do.

Royce was led through the arched gates, away from the city, away from his life, banished forever from everyone he'd ever known and loved and facing a journey before him that would be far worse than death.

The Pits, Royce thought. *Better to have died.*

CHAPTER SEVEN

Royce stumbled, shoved from behind, and bumped roughly into the group of boys as they were all herded onto the ship's long ramp. One eye still swollen shut, his head and body still killing him from all the lumps and bruises, Royce did not think he could feel any worse—until he finished climbing the ramp and set foot on board the ship. It rocked violently in the choppy waters, and as it lurched and he bumped into boys to the left and right of him, he received sharp elbows in the ribs and kidneys in return. He did not know which was worse: the elbows, or the sudden feeling of nausea.

Royce winced as the soldier grabbed him roughly from behind and threw him forward. He tried to turn and swing back, but he could not, his wrists still bound tightly behind him.

Still reeling from the events of the last few hours, still trying to process how his life had changed so dramatically so quickly, Royce tried to snap out of it, to take in the scene around him as best he could. As much as he felt like dying after being separated from Genevieve, from everyone he loved, his survival instincts kicked in, and he knew that if he wasn't on alert, he would get killed on this ship.

He looked around and saw hundreds of boys being prodded aboard, some appearing innocent, as shocked and disoriented as he, while others looked like professional criminals. Many of them, he noticed, were taller, broader, older, with rough stubble, prominent scars, shaved heads, and a look that told him that they'd kill over nothing. Even the boys his age looked prematurely aged, as if life had had its way with them.

It was a sea of desperate faces, of boys and men who knew they were being shipped off to their deaths and who had nothing left to lose.

The plank was raised behind him, slammed shut, and Royce felt his apprehension deepen, a heavy knot forming at the base of his throat, as he was shoved forward, deeper into the ship. He turned and watched the soldiers sever the ropes keeping the ship at shore, and all of a sudden, the ship began to move.

Royce lost his balance as the ship lurched forward. He looked out as the land began to get farther away and saw the docks were filled with bustling people—none of whom even looked their way to say goodbye. This ship, it seemed, was filled with people who were expendable. As they gained even more distance from shore, Royce knew that his life was about to change forever.

The waters became rougher as they left the harbor, and Royce struggled to gain his balance with his hands still bound behind him. The crowd became even thicker as all the boys surged forward, so thick he could barely breathe, the stench of unbathed men overwhelming. The ship groaned with all the weight; it seemed as if there were too many people on board to survive the ship ride. Maybe that was the point, Royce realized. Maybe they wanted to kill some of them off.

Indeed, Royce looked around and noticed several boys lying on the deck, unmoving. They were being trampled over casually by the masses, as still more people moved forward on the ship. He marveled that these boys were so hardened that they did not care about stepping on others, and he wondered why the boys lying down on deck weren't crying out in pain.

And then he realized. He looked down and saw the eyes wide open, and he knew with a chill that they were dead. Whether they had died from being trampled or from something else, he could not tell. One of them, he noticed, had a small dagger lodged in his chest. Royce glanced around at the hardened faces all around him and wondered which one might be responsible. From the looks of them, it could have been any of them. And probably, sadly, over nothing at all.

Royce felt more on guard than ever, realizing his troubles had not even begun. He was on a ship full of professional criminals, boys who were being sent to their deaths, who were desperate, who would kill over something small—or over nothing at all.

"Forward!" yelled a rough voice.

Royce felt a boot in the small of his back, and he stumbled forward as he was kicked. He slammed his head onto a wooden beam, the pain blinding, and he felt himself squeezed in from all sides. Suddenly the ship was hit by a wave, and icy spray rushed over the sides and across the ship, dousing Royce, shocking him fully awake. It was freezing, and the salt water stung his wounds. The water sloshed on the deck beneath his feet and he lost his footing and suddenly fell flat on his back, slamming his head on the wooden deck, unable to gain his balance with his hands bound behind his back.

The next thing Royce knew he felt the pain of a heavy boot stepping on his stomach; panic flooded him as he realized he might be trampled to death. Someone stepped on his leg, another person on his arm, and Royce looked up and saw another boot coming for his face and braced himself for the pain to follow.

Suddenly Royce felt hands on his back and was yanked back to his feet just before he was stepped on. He looked over to see a boy about his age, with sad, sunken green eyes and wavy black hair down to his chin. He did not look like the others here, Royce was surprised to see; his eyes were filled with kindness and intelligence, and he seemed to be of noble breeding.

He smiled wide, showing perfect teeth.

"Close call," he remarked.

Royce stared back, shocked, as he breathed a sigh of relief.

"You saved me," Royce said, stunned. "Why?"

He grinned.

"Mark's my name," he replied, "and I hate to see them trample people. I figured it would be a shame to let you die before you even had a chance to make it down below."

Royce nodded back with gratitude and was about to thank him—when a moment later, Mark himself was shoved across the deck by several guards. Royce tried to follow, but quickly lost him in the thickening crowd.

Royce felt guards grab him from behind, yank back his arms, and he wondered briefly if they were about to break them as the pain became more and more intense. His heart quickened as he saw a sharp knife. Were they going to stab him? What had he done?

To his surprise and relief they instead sliced the ropes binding his wrists; all around him they sliced the ropes of all the boys. Royce immediately held his wrists out before him, rubbing them, purple from being restrained, so grateful to have them free. He wondered if things were going to turn for the better.

But then he was kicked again, and a moment later he found himself flying down into the gaping hole leading below deck.

Royce dropped several feet, flailing through the air, and finally landed in the darkness, hitting the ground hard.

He slowly rose and looked around, as more and more boys were thrown in all around him. It was dim down here, this hold lit only by the light filtering down through the slats above. He saw the faces of the boys already amassed down here, hundreds of them on hammocks, hundreds standing, and hundreds more sleeping on the floor. He had never seen so many people packed into such a small space in his life. It was airless down here, and the stench was overwhelming.

More and more boys were being thrown through the hold. Trying to get away from the flying bodies, Royce made his way deeper inside, stepping over people carefully. He suddenly heard a dark laugh behind him.

"What are you avoiding them for, boy?" came a voice. "They been dead a long time."

Royce turned to see the menacing faces of a group of boys behind him, and watched as one of them, a tall boy with a big belly and dark, beady eyes, reached down, picked up one of the boys and held him to Royce's face. Royce recoiled as he saw the boy's face was covered in boils, his eyes wide open, his tongue hanging out of his mouth.

The boy gave a grim laugh.

"Don't think it's not coming for you, too," he warned. "They don't send us down here to live—they send us down to die."

Royce felt his apprehension deepen as a fresh wave of boys were thrown down and the mob pushed him forward. He pushed his way as deep into the hold as he could, desperate to get free, hoping to find a way back up. He slipped as the ship rocked, and he heard shouts and saw a fight break out in a dark corner of the hold. Above his head in the cramped space came the sound of thousands of heavy footsteps, floorboards creaking, as if the weight of the world were above him. He broke out into a sweat from the claustrophobic feeling down here; he felt as if he had been plunged into a vision of hell.

Royce rubbed his wrists again, thrilled to have them free of the binds, and wondering if he could somehow make it back above. Better to die up above, he figured, than down here.

He looked up ahead and saw one of the boys with the same idea, climbing, trying to get out of the hold and go above. Yet Royce watched in horror as he suddenly heard the thwack of a spear and saw the boy pierced in the chest. The boy fell back below with a thud, a spear in his chest, dead.

A soldier's face appeared above, glaring down at them, as if tempting anyone else to try.

Royce gave up on his idea and instead retreated to the darkest corner he could find, knowing for now he just needed to survive. He finally found a hammock, deep in the darkest corner, in which a boy lay unnaturally. Royce looked closely and as he suspected, the boy was dead, eyes wide open, a confused expression across his face, as if wondering how he could die here.

Royce tentatively reached up, pried the boy's stiff fingers off the net, and rolled him off the hammock. Royce hated to do it, and he braced himself as the body fell and landed on the floor with a thud. He had no other choice. The boy was dead now, and this hammock would do him no good.

But then a horrible thought crossed his mind: had the boy been killed in this hammock because someone else had wanted it?

Royce had no choice. He needed to get up off the ground, off the river of vomit and blood and death.

He pulled himself up, climbed into the hammock, and for the first time he felt a feeling of weightlessness. The aching in his feet and back momentarily subsided as he lay there, rocking with the ship.

He breathed deep. He wrapped himself in a ball as he swayed, the groaning of death all around him, and he knew, despite all that he had seen, his hell had not even begun.

CHAPTER EIGHT

Genevieve, alone in a small cell at the top of the fort's tower, leaned beside an open-aired window, looked down at the masses below, and wept. She was unable to hold back her tears any longer. She looked out and recalled how she had watched Royce disappear from view, dragged off by the knights, melting into the chaos of the mob as they had slowly wound their way toward the docks. Her heart had shattered. Watching Royce bound at the stake was more than she could take; yet even worse was hearing him sentenced to the Pits. Before her eyes, the man she loved most in the world, the one she had been about to wed, was being carried away to a certain death.

It wasn't fair. Royce had given up his life to save hers, had so fearlessly burst into the castle to risk it all. She flinched as she remembered Manfor's hands grabbing at her, as she recalled her sense of sheer terror. If Royce had not arrived when he had, she did not know what she would have done. Her life would have been over.

And yet maybe it was still over. Here she was, after all that, still trapped, still waiting to hear her fate. She recalled Lord Nors' words, and they rang in her ears like a death knell:

Yet your bride-to-be shall never be yours. She shall become the property of one of our nobles.

There was no outrunning them; there was *never* any outrunning them. The nobles ruled their lives, and always had. Disrespecting one of them meant a possible death—and killing one guaranteed it. And yet Royce had not hesitated to kill one for her sake.

Genevieve reeled at the thought. How much Royce had loved her; she had seen it in that moment. It had been so easy for him to give up his very life for hers. She wanted to risk it all for him, too, and what made her feel the worst of all was that she was trapped here, unable to help him.

A heavy iron bolt suddenly slid back on the other side of her door, shattering her silence, and Genevieve flinched in her solitary cell. There came the sound of the thick wooden door creaking as it was pulled open, and she saw two stone-faced soldiers awaiting her silently. Her heart fell. Were they coming to lead her to her death?

"You will be seen now," one announced gruffly.

They stood there in silence, waiting, yet she only stood there, frozen in terror. A part of her wanted to stay here, alone in this cell, a prisoner for the rest of her days. She was not ready to face the world, and certainly not the nobles. She wanted more time to process it all, and more time to think of Royce. Yet returning to her normal life, she knew, was no longer a possibility. She was the property of these nobles now, theirs to do with as they wished.

Genevieve took a deep breath in the stillness and took one step forward, then another. Walking toward these men was worse than walking to the gallows.

As they walked down the corridor, the door slamming behind her, one grabbed her roughly, too roughly, his calloused fingers digging into the soft flesh of her arm. Genevieve wanted to cry out in pain. But she did not. She would not give him the satisfaction.

He leaned in close, so close that she could feel his hot breath on her cheek.

"Your boyfriend killed my lord," he said. "He will suffer. You, too, will suffer—though in a different way. A longer, crueler way."

He jerked her, leading her down the twisting and turning corridors, the sound of their footsteps echoing on the stone, and as they went, Genevieve shuddered. She tried not to think of what lay awaiting her. How had everything turned out this way? This had begun as the happiest day of her life—and somehow had morphed into tragedy.

Genevieve glanced out the open windows as they passed by and saw the courtyard far below, the masses coming and going, all of them already back to their daily routine. She wondered how life could just go on like that, as if nothing had ever happened. For her, life had changed forever. Yet the world seemed to be unfazed.

As she looked down at the stone far below, she felt a sudden rush of hope. She *did* have one last power at her disposal, she realized: the power to end it all. All she had to do was break free of this soldier's grip, run and jump out the open-aired window. She could end it all.

She calculated how many steps it would take, whether he would catch her before she leapt, and whether the fall would be far enough to break her neck. Pondering this, she felt a perverse sense of joy. It was the one power she had left. It was the one thing she could do to show her solidarity to Royce. If Royce was going to die, she should die, too.

"What are you smiling about?" the guard hissed.

She didn't respond—she hadn't even realized she was smiling. Her actions would answer for her.

Heart pounding, Genevieve waited for his grip to loosen so she could yank her arm away and run. Yet, to her dismay, he only squeezed harder, never loosening it for one second.

Genevieve's heart fell as they turned down a new corridor, one with no windows. They reached a new door and as he ushered her inside, she realized her opportunity was lost.

Next time, she told herself.

Genevieve entered a vaulted chamber, dim and cool in here, with soaring ceilings. She was led to the center of the room by the two guards, who finally let go and stood a few feet away. She rubbed her arm from where he had grabbed it, relieved to have it free.

Facing Genevieve was a man, clearly a noble from the looks of him. He stood opposite her, a few feet away, and stared back with a cool, hard gaze. He seemed to examine her as if she were a statue, or an interesting piece of art which had been brought before him.

She felt an immediate sense of revulsion upon looking at him: he resembled Manfor. His brother, perhaps?

He stood there, with his fine chiseled looks, a man of perhaps twenty, an arrogant look on his face, not quite a scowl. Dressed in the finest of velvets, indicative of his position, he was flanked by two older men, dressed equally luxuriously. Behind these stood several attendants. His eyes were red, as though from crying, and his face was framed by longish, wavy brown hair. He'd be attractive, she thought, if his face wasn't puffed up by such arrogance and cruelty.

The boy stared coldly at her, and she locked her jaws and stared back at him, immune to his hate. She, after all, wanted no one's approval.

A long, heavy silence blanketed the room as they each stood there, staring in stony silence. The room was filled with the silent tension of grief, of blame, of anger, of vengeance. Almost nothing needed to be said.

Finally, the man spoke.

"Do you know who I am?" he asked. His voice was not unpleasant, smooth on the air, a voice of authority, of privilege, of entitlement.

She looked into his hard, brown eyes, studying them.

"Manfor's brother, I would assume," she replied, her voice scratchy from lack of use.

He shook his head.

"I *was* his brother," he corrected. "My brother is dead now, thanks to you."

His eyes narrowed in disapproval as he looked at her as if she had stabbed his brother herself. She wished she had. She wished she could take her beloved Royce's plight away from him, wished that he had not had to suffer because of her.

She desperately wanted to end this. Here, after all, was her enemy, standing before her. She furtively scanned the room, looking for any weapons—a sword she could draw, a dagger she could throw—anything to plunge into this man's heart. Her thought quickly turned to resolve. She noticed one of the guards, now looking away, had a dagger in his belt, at his waist, and she wondered if she could snatch it, wondered how quickly she could take the few steps and stab him before they could stop her.

"Did you hear what I asked you?"

She blinked and looked back at him as she snapped out of it, unaware that he'd been speaking.

"I said," he repeated, "my name is Altfor. And your precious Royce would lie dead right now if it weren't for the peasants. Indeed, nothing would give me greater pleasure than to watch him beheaded in the square. Yet ultimately, it does not matter. He will die regardless, albeit in a long, torturous way in the Pits. I suppose that is better off, though it does rob me of my satisfaction."

Genevieve burned with indignation while Altfor took a step closer. His sneer deepened.

"My brother's life was robbed from him," he seethed. "My *brother*. And by a poor peasant. It's *disgraceful*!" he yelled out, his words echoing off the walls and the floors, his anger lingering in the air.

He lowered his voice.

"And all for *you*," he concluded with contempt.

A heavy silence fell again. She had no intention of responding. She couldn't care less that he was angry—indeed, she wanted him to be. She wanted him to suffer, as she had suffered.

"Have you nothing to say?" he finally prodded.

A long silence remained between them, each staring back, each equally determined, until finally she spoke:

"What is it you would like me to say?" she asked.

His gaze hardened.

"That you are sorry. That you never meant for it to happen. That you are glad that Royce will die."

Genevieve clenched her jaws.

"None of those are true," she replied, her voice filled with a calm that she had not felt until now. "I am thrilled your brother is dead. He was a thief and a murderer and a rapist. He stole me away on the day of my wedding; he robbed me of the greatest joy of my life; and as a result of your brother's heinous actions, the man who loved me, the man who came to save me, is now an outcast. I regret only that your brother did not die sooner—and that I myself did not wield the blade."

Her words came out with anger and venom to match his, and she could see each one hurting him. She saw, too, his look of surprise. Clearly he had expected her to buckle—and she had not.

He stared back now with shock and, perhaps, with something close to respect.

"You are a willful girl, aren't you?" he said, slowly nodding. "Yes. That is what they say about you. A girl with much spirit. And yet, what use is spirit in the life of a girl? What shall your occupation be, after all? Wife. Mother. You shall be spending your days sewing and knitting, wiping the behind of babes. What purpose shall your spirit serve you then?"

She glowered.

"You tarnish a profession that is more noble than yours," she spat back. "You tarnish your own mother's profession—though from her handiwork, I am not surprised."

He frowned, clearly at a loss for words, and she stared back, silently fuming. She had in fact resolved to be a devoted wife and mother, and for her there was no greater calling. She had also resolved to train, to be a warrior in her own right; she was already finer with a sword than most of the boys. She had taken her fair share of the hunt, something other girls wouldn't do, and had truer aim with the arrow than most men she had met. Even Royce was not as accurate as she.

"The irony is," she continued, "if I had a fine bow and arrow at my disposal now, I would place the arrow between your eyes before you could finish speaking. Wife and mother are not exclusive talents," she replied. "I have other talents, too, which I would gladly display on you."

He stared back, clearly stunned.

Then, after what seemed like an eternity, he broke into a smile.

"They underestimated you, indeed," he replied. "My brother snatched you as a sport to discard at day's end. He clearly had no idea whom he had chosen."

He examined her up and down with a new look, one that clearly held respect, and perhaps even admiration. She did not like the look; she preferred it when he looked upon her with scorn only.

"I am above your station," he continued. "And yet I see something in you. My brother happened upon you by mistake; I shall happen upon you by choice. You cannot be killed, if we wish to appease the peasantry. Nor can we set you free, after all you've been involved in, whether willingly or not."

He sighed.

"So I will take your hand in marriage," he concluded, as if bargaining at a farm stand and buying a particularly fine sheep for the night's meal.

Genevieve stared back, flabbergasted.

"Consider it a lucky fortune that I found you here today," he continued. "Endless women in this countryside would die to be my bride; you have won. Count your blessings. You shall walk into a life of nobility, and I shall settle this matter on my father's behalf and bring peace to the peasantry. We shall put all this unpleasant business behind us, for the sake of our families, and the sake of our kingdom."

As he spoke, Genevieve felt the life slowly slipping from her, felt her body go numb with shock. She was not surprised that he would have her; indeed, she had expected to be raped and tortured by him, if not killed. What surprised her were his words. How soaring, how elegant they were. He had complimented her when he had not needed to; he had even spoken admiringly of her. He would not take her as his plaything, as she had expected, but as his *wife*. As a member of his family. As a noble.

It was all, of course, supremely insulting given what had just been done to the love of her life, to the man she loved most. Yet what bothered her the most was that there was also something complimentary in it. She wished there hadn't been; it would make all this easier to accept as punishment. Despite herself, despite her intense hatred for him, despite wanting to stab him through the heart, she had to admit to herself that there was a part of her, deep down inside, that was surprised by him and that maybe even admired him, too. Despite his arrogance, he was cut from a shockingly different cloth than his brother; the contrast was startling, and completely caught her off guard.

Genevieve felt ill, feeling a sense of betrayal for even thinking these thoughts, and she hated herself for it. There was only one way, she knew, to drive away these less-than-negative thoughts about him from her mind: she scanned the room again for the dagger. Her heart beat faster as she prepared to lunge for it.

He laughed, surprising her.

"You will never reach that dagger," he said.

She flinched and looked back to see him staring back at her, smiling.

"Look carefully," he added. "It is strapped in on all sides. Try to draw it, and you will get stuck. And you forget this."

She followed his hand and saw it resting on a dagger in his own belt.

She reddened, feeling foolish, knowing her mind had been read. Altfor was much more perceptive than she had given him credit for.

He looked at his guards, his eyes suddenly cold again.

"Take her away."

Suddenly the rough hands were grabbing her again, yanking her arms, pulling her away. She fully expected Altfor to order them to take her to the gallows, to order her killed for attempting to kill him. But instead, he gave them a command that shocked her more than sentencing her to death ever could:

"Have her cleaned up," he said. "And prepared to wed."

CHAPTER NINE

Raymond had always thought of himself as the clever one. He was the eldest of the brothers, without Lofen's tendency to get into fights or Garet's impulsiveness. As for Royce... well, Royce was different. Any idiot could see that.

"What I need to see," Raymond said as they made their way across the heathland outside the village, "is a way that we can all get out of this alive."

"What we need to do is gather up all the men of our family and take the castle," Lofen said.

Raymond laughed bitterly at that. "Unless I miscounted at the last feast day, there's not enough of our kin to take a badger's den from it, let alone a fort like that."

That was the hardest part of it to accept. They'd fought to distract the guards at the castle, but hadn't been able to save Royce, had barely been able to get away themselves. They'd tried to be there for the trial, had been in the crowds at the docks, and each time, there had been too many men, too many guards to do anything but die trying to help.

"Then we need to go home," Garet said. Of course the youngest would want to run back and hide behind their mother's skirts. A part of Raymond wanted to as well, but he knew it wouldn't work like that.

"If we go home, we'll find knights waiting for us," Raymond said. "We need to stay clear until things die down, find a safe place out in the hills, try and work out what happens next."

Would they flee over the sea? Would they go up into the far wilds of the country, where they said that there were still Picti left over from the days before true men had come to it? How long could they run? How long could they hide?

No, Raymond thought, in spite of it all, his brothers were right. They needed to find a way to help Royce. If they could get a force to the place where Royce had been taken, the Red Isle, then maybe they could get him out, and with him there, maybe they could do more.

"How many cousins and friends do we actually have?" Raymond asked the others.

They started to total them up.

"There's Aunt Willa's boys," Garet said, "and maybe we could call a meet, get men interested."

"As good as an invitation to the Duke's forces," Lofen said. "Now, I've got friends who like a good fight..."

Boys who were good with their fists, not men with swords. Even so, Raymond was willing to accept all the help that they could get for this.

"We have to risk the village," he declared to the others. "We'll pick up men there, find someone with a boat. We might not have enough to take the castle, but I reckon we can find enough to sneak our brother off of an island."

They started off in the direction of the village, keeping low, staying away from the road as best they could. Raymond could see the village in the distance now, and he hoped that he would be able to find enough help there. They couldn't leave Royce to his fate.

Could they get there and find that help without running into trouble, though? The answer to that came in the sound of hooves thundering over the wet ground.

"Run!" Raymond yelled, even before the riders came into view. There were at least a dozen of them, both true knights and sergeants at arms.

They ran, but even at full pelt, even knowing the land better, they couldn't outrun horses. The dozen that chased them circled them, riding round as if preparing for a joust.

"His lordship says you're to be brought in alive," one of the knights called out. "Surrender and you won't be killed."

Raymond drew his sword. He and his brothers might not be noble warriors, but they'd trained every day nonetheless.

"You'll have to take us if you want us," he called out.

The knights came in, thrusting down with the butts of their spears, using them like clubs. Raymond didn't feel the need to hold back like that, cutting up at one of them and feeling his sword scrape off the man's armor.

He saw Garet brought down first, laid out by the swinging blow of a spear. Lofen lasted a little longer, managing to drag a man from his horse but quickly finding that there were three more there to grab him.

Raymond ran in to help, swinging his sword at the nearest of the men. He struck hard, feeling the sword bite deeply as it connected. He spun to face the next of them, and parried a blow, cutting back and feeling the scrape of steel through flesh.

He heard the sound of hooves nearby and started to turn again, but this time he was too slow. Raymond felt the jarring thud as the haft of a spear struck him behind the ear. The world seemed to swim and then Raymond was down on his knees, his sword clattering from his hand. Rough hands grabbed his arms, dragging them behind his back to tie them. By then though, he was already sliding into unconsciousness…

*

Raymond slid in and out of wakefulness, feeling the jolting of the horse that he'd been thrown over. In the moments when he was conscious, he was able to make out his brothers, slung across the back of other horses.

Ahead, he could see the castle of the lord, the portcullis open, the drawbridge down to receive them. The horses rode inside, the knights there seizing his arms and dragging him down from the one he was thrown over. They dragged him and the others to an iron-bound door set at the bottom of a series of steps. A guard there sat on a stool, keys hanging from his fingers.

"You caught them, then," he said. "His lordship said to throw them into the main dungeon and see if anyone knifes them."

The knight holding Raymond nodded. "Pretty boys like these, they'll be lucky if that's the worst that happens to them."

The jailor dragged open the door and the knights led Raymond and his brothers into the dark space beyond. There were individual cells there near the door, some of them with occupants, along with a room where screams came from behind the door in a way that sent shivers down Raymond's spine.

There was a door beyond that, which the jailor opened cautiously, stepping back as if expecting someone to burst out. There were steps leading further down beyond, into an unlit space.

"This is where we throw the people we want to forget," the jailor said. "Enjoy it. I know they'll enjoy you."

The knights threw Garet and Lofen through, and then it was Raymond's turn. They cut the ropes on his wrists and then shoved him into the space beyond the door. He half tumbled, half ran down the stairs, and landed in a heap at the bottom.

In the darkness there, he could make out the eyes on him, and he knew that if he and his brothers didn't stick together they would be just as dead as if they'd been executed.

CHAPTER TEN

Royce sat in the hold beneath the ship, curled up in a dark corner with his hands wrapped around his knees, and opened his eyes slowly, awakened from a fitful sleep. He peered out, on guard immediately, as he had all the time since he'd been thrown down here. His eyes adjusted slowly as he stared out at a room filled with chaos and death.

What he saw made him wish he had never woken. It was as grim as ever, more people dead down here than alive, bodies covering the floors, covered in boils and vomit. The stench was nearly unbearable. He marveled that more and more boys had been shoved down here, a seemingly endless stream. This hold was used as a dumping ground, presumably for punishments up above, or just for the unlucky ones.

All the hammocks were filled with kids, some alert, others snoring, some staring blankly at the ceiling, all of them swaying more wildly than usual as Royce felt waves pound the boat. He wished he was in one now. Yet he had learned long ago to vacate the hammock in favor of the floor. He had seen too many kids killed by sleeping in hammocks, others creeping up on them and stabbing them for their sleeping place. They'd been helpless to resist while trapped in the hammock's net. Royce had long since kept to the floor, finding the darkest corner he could and sleeping with his hands across his knees, his back to the corner so no one would attack him. It was safer this way.

Once a day the guards opened the hatch, letting in a burst of ocean air and light. At first Royce thought that meant they would let them all go up and have a little freedom to move. But then he saw huge sacks being opened and dumped down, heard the scattering of what sounded like sand on the floor, and as he'd watched the boys dive for it, like savage animals, grabbing fistfuls, he realized: grain. It was their feeding time.

The boys shoved it in their mouths, shoving each other aside, punching, elbowing, blood landing in the grain. It was a brutal competition for survival—and it happened once a day. The guards always left the hatch open long enough to watch, grinning down at the spectacle, then slammed it shut.

Royce had told himself he would never participate in that mosh pit. Yet after a day his hunger got the best of him and he dove in with the others, grabbing a handful of grain just as another boy tried to pry it from his hands. They fought over it briefly, until Royce yanked it away and the boy moved on to some other place. Royce gulped it down immediately. It was crunchy and tasteless and it hardly nourished him. But it was something. He learned his lesson, too—the following day he would try to grab two fistfuls, and ration it.

It had been a grim existence down here, one of survival, day after day of watching for the hatch to open, grabbing whatever food he could, and retreating back to his corner. He had seen too many boys die; he had tolerated too long the perpetual stench. He had watched as too many bullies roamed the hold, predators, waiting until other boys appeared too weak to fight—then pouncing on them and taking whatever meager possessions they had. It was constantly unsettling.

Royce barely slept. He was troubled constantly by nightmares, images of being stabbed in his sleep, of floating in a coffin in a sea of blood, of being engulfed by the massive waves of the ocean. These, in turn, morphed into nightmares of Genevieve, of her being raped by the nobles of the castle, of his arriving too late to save her. Of his brothers and family back home, their house and fields burned to the ground, all of them having moved on, having long forgotten him.

He always woke in a cold sweat. He did not know which was worse these days: to sleep or to wake.

On this day, though, as Royce woke, he immediately sensed something was different. He felt his stomach dropping more severely than usual, heard the crashing of the waves against the deck more strongly, heard the high-pitched whistling of the wind, and he knew right away that a storm had come. And no normal storm. But a storm that might change everything.

Panicked shouting came from somewhere high above, followed by the sound of boots running across the deck, more urgent than before, and a moment later, to Royce's surprise, the hatch was thrown open. It was never thrown open this early in the day.

He sat up, alert.

Something was wrong.

He stared at the open sky, such a luxury these days, and saw it was thick with dark, angry clouds, moving too quickly; he saw rain lashing down, so severe it was sideways. He did not even need to see it—the sound hit him first. He stared at the open hatch but did not see several strong hands opening it, as usual. Instead, it had opened by itself—yanked up by a gust of wind.

Royce watched in amazement as the hundred-pound wooden hatch suddenly lifted, all by itself, and went spinning and flying into the air, as if it were a child's toy. He gulped. If winds could do that to something so heavy, what could they do to a man?

Indeed, the sound of roaring winds drowned out everything, a sound so intense that it struck terror in him even far below. It sounded as if it were tearing the ship to pieces. As he watched, a plank of wood went flying up into the air, right off the deck itself.

Suddenly, his stomach plummeted, as the ship dropped and there came the crashing of an enormous wave against the hull. He felt as if he had dropped fifty feet. He was amazed the ship did not capsize.

Royce looked at the other boys, their faces finally visible in the sunlight, all of them appearing full of hope to see the sky—yet also full of terror at the storm. Freedom finally sat right before them, a chance to climb up, to go above and get out of this hellhole.

Yet none of them dared move. All sat frozen in terror of the storm.

A heavy rope suddenly flew down into the hatch, landing like a coiled snake with a thud. There appeared the face of a guard, clutching a beam for dear life and scowling down as he leaned over.

"Man the decks!" he cried, struggling to be heard over the wind. "All of you up here now!"

No one moved.

He looked irate.

"Come now, or I will come down there and kill every last one of you myself!"

Still, none moved.

A second later, a spear came flying through the air, and Royce watched in horror as it punctured the chest of a boy right beside him. The boy cried out, pinned to the floor of the hold, instantly dead.

Two guards jumped down, raised their swords, grabbed the closest boys and stabbed them in the chest.

As the boys fell, the guards turned and looked at the rest.

All the other boys jumped into action, rushing for the ropes, climbing up and out of the hold. Royce went with them. Death surely awaited him up there—but at least it would be a cleaner death. Maybe he'd get lucky and a wave would wash him out to sea and he could leave this entire nightmare behind him.

Royce looked up and watched as the first boy climbed up, struggling, weak with malnourishment. He finally reached the deck and as he did, he grabbed hold of the railing, pulled himself up, and crawled over the edge. He did so awkwardly, raising his legs in the air. Royce watched with horror as the boy lost his grip and flew through the air, lifted by the wind like a plank of wood. He spun again and again, his shrieking drowned out by the wind, until he flew over the rail and into the sea.

Royce's apprehension deepened. His turn finally came, and he grabbed the rope firmly, his heart pounding in his ears, and climbed up one inch at a time. The noise of the wind grew louder as he reared his head, and he finally grabbed hold of the deck, hands shaking.

The noise was unbearable up here, the visibility almost zero, and as he crawled over the edge, out of the hold for the first time in weeks, he held on for dear life. He lost his grip and slipped, his body sliding across the deck, then grabbed it again. He learned from the others' mistakes, keeping his body low and crawling along the deck.

Royce grabbed hold of a peg firmly attached to the deck and crawled against the wind, fighting for every foot, until he finally found a spot where he could brace himself. He grabbed hold of two pegs, one in each hand, and braced his feet against two pegs behind him, taking shelter behind a high mast. He felt stable here, even as the boat rocked violently from side to side and rose and plummeted, waves crashing all around him.

"Bring in that sail!" yelled a soldier, shouting over the wind.

Royce looked up at a violently flapping sail high overhead, its weight bending the mast until it nearly broke. He felt a soldier's spear prod him in the back and knew that if he did not jump into action, he would meet another death.

Royce stood and grabbed the mast, hugging it with all he had. Holding onto it with one hand he then reached out and grabbed the dangling rope, pulling it in. The coarse, wet rope slipped in his hand, yet as he yanked, several other boys joined him, they, too, prodded by the soldiers. Together, they all yanked, and foot by foot they managed to lower the sail. As it came in, the thick mast stopped bending, and the ship righted and rocked less violently.

A fierce gust of wind blew through and Royce held the mast tight. The boy beside him, though, did not react as quickly, and before he could grab hold he lost his balance and went stumbling backward, landing on his back on the deck. A wave hit, the ship turned sideways, and Royce watched as the boy slid all the way across the deck, a dozen other boys sliding with him, until they all fell overboard, shrieking.

Royce looked out and saw an army of whitecaps dotting the seas, and he knew he would not see them again. His dread deepened. He felt increasingly he would not survive.

"Tie in that canvas!" shouted a soldier.

Royce realized the canvas sail was flapping wildly over his head and he reached up and grabbed it, trying to tie it down. It slipped from his hands, but he finally managed to grab hold of it with his arm and hold it tight. He grabbed the rope that was flailing in the wind and wrapped it around the canvas again and again, tying it to the mast.

The ship suddenly rocked and turned sideways again, and as Royce held on for dear life, he watched as several boys went slipping the other way, heading for the rail. He recognized amongst them the boy with the wavy black hair, who had spared him all those weeks before in that stampede: Mark. There he was, sliding, trying to grab hold of anything he could, but unable to. In moments he would be overboard.

Royce could not let him die.

As risky as it was, Royce let go of the mast with one hand and reached out for him.

"HERE!" he shouted.

Mark looked over, reached out, and as he slid past, he just managed to grab hold of his hand. He held on tight, looking up at Royce with fear and desperation in his eyes, and most of all, gratitude. Royce held on with all his might, not letting him slide back the other way as the ship turned nearly vertical. The other boys, though, shrieking, fell overboard.

Royce held on with shaking hands, feeling as though all his muscles would burst, praying for the ship to right itself. He was barely able to hold the mast with his other hand, his grip slipping. He knew that in but another moment, he too, would go overboard.

"Let me go!" Mark yelled. "You're not going to make it!"

But Royce shook his head, knowing he had to save him. He owed it to him.

Finally, the ship righted itself, and Royce felt his muscles relax as Mark was able to hurry over and grab the mast beside him. They both stood there, hugging the mast, breathing hard.

"I owe you," Mark called out.

Royce shook his head.

"We're even."

Royce heard a cry behind him, and he turned to see one of the bullies from below raise his dagger and stab an unsuspecting boy in the back; he then grabbed a sack from the dead boy's waist and stuffed it on his own. Royce shook his head, marveling that these predators would attack even in the midst of such a storm.

Yet a moment later a huge wave doused the ship, and that bully, in turn, went flying overboard into the sea.

The wave doused Royce. For a moment he was completely submerged in freezing water, and then the wave left just as quickly, leaving him gasping for air, trying to catch his breath. He blinked and wiped water from his eyes and hair and was relieved to see that Mark was still there, holding on. He felt colder than ever, and as he looked out at the angry sea before them, filled with whitecaps, he knew it would only get worse. He realized then that staying up here, above deck, would mean certain death.

"We're not going to make it up here!" Royce called out to Mark.

But before he could finish, another wave came crashing down on them; again they held on, yet as the wave disappeared, Royce watched it take several men—including the soldier who had been standing guard over him.

"We have to get down below!" Royce called.

Royce looked out at the remaining soldiers and saw they were preoccupied with staying alive themselves; he doubted they would notice him disappear, or have time to go on a manhunt below.

"Let's go!" Mark called back.

They both let go of the mast and raced for the open hold below—but as they did, another huge wave came crashing down on them. They fell flat against the wooden deck and went sliding as the boat turned nearly sideways. Royce flailed underwater, aiming for the open hold, trying to steer himself—and a moment later, to his relief, he felt himself falling into it as the wave passed by. He felt a body land beside him, and he knew Mark had made it, too.

Royce landed not on a hard wood floor, as he had expected, but rather in several feet of water. The hold, he realized with dread, was filling up.

Royce stood and saw the water down here was a few feet deep, sloshing around. He saw something float past and felt it bump against his leg, and he looked down and saw it was a dead body, one of the many boys who had died below. He surveyed the hold and saw, to his horror, the water was filled with floating corpses. The chances of survival down here were slim, too, he realized. Yet up above it was impossible.

The waters rose higher and higher, soon up to his waist. Royce knew that when they reached the top, he would be floating back on deck, and his life would be over.

He reached out, grabbed onto a peg on the wall and onto the rope of an old hammock, bracing himself, while Mark did the same. They stood there and waited, watching the waters rise, and as Royce saw death all around him, he wondered just how he would die.

CHAPTER ELEVEN

Genevieve felt the tears slide down her cheeks as her new handmaidens, encircling her, fitted her into her wedding dress. She looked down at it in despair: it might as well have been a funeral gown. With each pull of the cord, tying the corset tighter around her waist, she felt as if another string of her life were being pulled, cutting her off from the future she had imagined with Royce, and sentencing her to a marriage that would be her death.

"Do not cry now, it is unbecoming of a bride," came a voice.

Genevieve was only dimly aware of the girls attending her, a half dozen of them, all busy preparing as she sat on a bench in the stone chamber in this fort. Some worked on her shoes—tall, leather things that strapped to her knees—while others fixed her hair, trimmed her dress, rubbed oils into her skin, and applied makeup. It was the girl wiping her cheeks with the cool rag, wiping away her tears, who had spoken to her.

Genevieve looked over and saw the girl staring back at her, a few years older, with long, curly black hair, green eyes, and a kind face. She was surprised at her look of compassion, the first she had seen since entering this fort. She covered up Genevieve's tears with a dab of makeup, treating Genevieve as if she were a doll. For these people, Genevieve knew, it was all about appearances.

"It's not as bad as you think, you know," the girl went on. "After all, you're marrying into nobility; it could be worse."

Genevieve closed her eyes and shook her head.

"I am *not* marrying him," Genevieve insisted, her voice sounding far off to her.

The girl gave her a confused look.

"He may be marrying me," Genevieve clarified, "and there is nothing I can do about it. Yet I shall not consider myself wed to him."

The girls all giggled around her.

Genevieve frowned, determined to express her seriousness.

"My heart belongs to another," she added, to cement her point.

Finally the girls' expressions turned serious, as they gave each other worried glances.

The girl attending Genevieve's makeup turned to the other girls and shooed them off. They all left, concern etched across their faces. Genevieve wondered who they would run and tell. She did not care.

Soon they were alone, just Genevieve and the girl, and the room fell silent. The girl continued to look at Genevieve with wise and understanding eyes.

"My name is Moira," she said. "I am wife to Ned, the youngest brother of the man you will wed. I guess that shall make us sisters?" She smiled weakly. "I've always wanted a sister."

Genevieve did not know how to reply; Moira seemed kind enough, yet she did not wish anyone in this fort to be her family.

Moira took a deep breath as she came around behind her and began tying up her hair.

"Allow me to give you a word of advice, having lived in this family for too many years," she added. "They will do whatever they have to, to stay in power. They do not choose brides meaninglessly. And to marry them is like a small death."

Genevieve turned to her, struck by her honesty, and for the first time, she really listened to her.

"They marry not for love, these people, but for power. They marry to survive. It is all part of a game for them."

Genevieve frowned.

"I do not wish to understand them," she replied. "I do not care for any of their games. I wish only for the man I love to be returned to me."

Moira shot her a look of disapproval.

"But you *must* understand them," she countered. "That is your only chance to survive. You must enter their sick, twisted minds, and discover what it is that drives them."

She sighed, tightening her hair.

"I like you," she continued. "I'd like to see you survive. So let me give you one word of advice: do not let anyone else hear you profess your love for another. These men, if they hear you, may very well cut out your tongue as soon as marry you."

Genevieve felt her chest tighten, sensing Moira spoke the truth. This place was even more brutal than she had imagined, and her sense of dread increased.

Moira stepped closer, glanced around, and lowered her voice as if to make sure no one was listening.

"*No one* within these walls can be trusted," she continued. "Accept your lot. The best way to defeat them is to embrace them. Embrace your new title, your new power. Become the worm from within. Give them time. Allow them to think you love them. Allow their guard to lower. And then, when they are comfortable, strike."

Genevieve stared back, shocked she would be so frank. She wondered what Moira had suffered to feel the way she had.

"Remember," Moira said, "there are many ways to achieve an objective."

The door suddenly opened, and several more attendants appeared. They stood at attention, clearly awaiting Genevieve's departure.

"The wedding party awaits," one announced, grim-faced.

Knowing the time had come, Genevieve looked at Moira, who nodded back knowingly. Together, they walked slowly from the room, Moira holding her train.

Fresh tears came with each step Genevieve took. This was not the way she had ever imagined walking down the aisle.

Genevieve walked the gloomy stone corridors, lit by torches, winding her way, and as she went she looked for open-aired windows, for a way to jump—but she found none. Feeling as if she were marching to her death, she wondered where Royce was at this moment. She wondered if he was dreaming of her, too. She wondered if she would ever lay eyes upon him again.

She found herself led through a vaulted opening and into a huge, vaulted chamber. She was surprised to see hundreds of nobles in attendance, seated in pews. At the end of the aisle awaited an altar, framed by stained glass. Beside it stood a priest.

And there, waiting, was Altfor. Her groom-to-be.

Genevieve took a deep breath and resolved not to go. She would strangle him before she agreed to marry.

Yet right before she crossed the threshold of the door, she felt a strong grip on her arm. She turned and looked over to see Moira shaking her head, as if reading her mind.

"Wed him," she whispered. "Love him. Or allow him to think that you do. And then when the time is right, we can kill them. We can kill them all."

Genevieve stood there, trembling, struggling with what to do. This was her last chance to turn and run, to let them imprison or kill her.

"If you love Royce," Moira added, "climb the path of power. That is the only way to freedom for you both."

Moira gestured for Genevieve to walk into the room.

Genevieve stood there, her mind reeling, and she sensed Moira was right. She had no other way to help Royce. And for Royce, she would do anything.

Slowly, one step at a time, a pit in her stomach, Genevieve began to walk. She walked down the aisle, the room thick with incense and filtered sunlight, and she looked up at her waiting groom, at her waiting life. And she died inside.

Yet she forced herself to take one step after the next. And as she did, she thought to herself:

Royce. This is for you.

CHAPTER TWELVE

Royce slowly opened his eyes to the gentle sound of sloshing water, and he looked about, disoriented. He was lying face down on the upper deck of the ship, his face in an inch of water, lapping gently against his cheek. Water splashed over his chin, up his cheek, and into his ear, and he wondered briefly if he was dead.

Royce lifted his head slowly, half of it dripping, the other half dry and sunburned, and blinked several times as he wiped salt-encrusted water from his eyelids. His head was splitting, his throat parched, and his body felt like one big bruise.

He slowly rose to his hands and knees, breathing hard, wondering what had happened, and wondering how he had survived the storm.

The silence was most unnerving of all. During these past moons the ship had been clamorous, filled with the sounds of boys groaning, shrieking, fighting, dying. It had been filled with the ubiquitous sounds of soldiers relentlessly ordering, whipping, beating, killing. It had been filled with ever-present sounds of agony and misery and death.

Yet now it was silent, still. Royce looked out and saw the sun breaking over the sky, a dull red, and it felt as if he were the last man alive in the world. How had he survived? How had the ship survived?

He looked around and saw it was badly listing, limping along in the open waters, which were now calm as a lake. Royce felt something bump against his knee, looked down—and wished he hadn't. There was a corpse, a boy who looked to be his age, lifeless, eyes open to the sky as he floated across the deck, bumping against him.

Royce turned and scanned the deck and, in the breaking dawn, saw dozens more bodies floating, some face up, some face down, all sloshing on the ship. He felt a wave of revulsion. It was a floating graveyard.

Royce shook his head, trying to push the image from his mind. The storm had taken nearly all of them. He closed his eyes and tried not to hear the screams, tried not to think of all the faces, of all the boys who had died, now somewhere overboard, carried off in the wind and waves.

And yet he supposed he should be grateful. If things had stayed as they were, if he had stayed down below, he would surely have died eventually, of plague or the dagger, if not starvation. This storm at least had allowed him to get out from below; indeed, he turned and looked over at the hatch below, saw its edges been shattered, and was shocked to see it was now entirely filled with water. Floating up from out of it were several dead bodies, sloshing across deck.

Slowly, there emerged sounds of life, a distant splashing, and Royce turned to see one boy rising to his hands and knees from the deck as the sun rose in the sky. Then came another.

And another.

One by one, signs of life began to return.

Soldiers began to rise, too, one at a time, and soon dozens of members of the ship came back to life. As the sky lightened, Royce realized with a combination of relief and dread that he was not the only one. Somehow, despite it all, others had survived.

As the new day broke Royce looked out and was amazed at how calm the sky was, how calm the waters were, as if a storm had never happened. The water was shockingly still, no sound audible save for the slightest lapping against the hold. It was like sailing on a lake.

As Royce looked he was startled to see something else: there, on the horizon, was a landmass. He spotted craggy black cliffs rising up from the sea, as if a sulfur monster had emerged and hardened. It looked to be a bleak, unforgiving place, yet still, Royce's heart quickened: it was land, at least. The first land he had seen in weeks.

And clearly, their destination.

"Slaves, get back to work!" called out a rough voice.

Royce sensed a commotion behind him, and found himself pushed, stumbling forward. He couldn't believe it. Already the soldiers were rounding up the boys, ordering them around as if nothing had changed, despite the carnage around them. Royce wondered how many of them had survived, if the boys now outnumbered the guards and could stage a revolt. Yet as he looked around Royce saw a surprising number of guards had lived, more and more of them seeming to rise from the dead. And this ship was in too bad a shape to take anywhere.

Royce soon found himself herded with a group of several dozen boys, a dozen soldiers behind them, being shoved toward the bow. The soldiers wanted to make them work the sails, to steer the ship; yet the sails were tattered and the wheel had blown off. So instead, they shoved and pushed Royce and the others toward several shattered benches affixed to the edge of the deck.

"Oars!" they commanded.

Royce found himself shoved roughly onto the remains of a bench, a huge oar placed into his hand. He looked over the ship and saw the oar descended thirty feet into the water, and he followed as the others reached forward with their oars, then pulled back, tugging at the water. Royce felt his arms, weak from hunger, shake.

Slowly, the ship began to move. It had been drifting, directionless, yet now it moved straight ahead, toward the distant isle. Royce heard the crack of a whip, saw one of the boys nearby lashed, and as he heard him cry out in pain, Royce rowed harder. The guards were merciless, even in a state like this.

There came a commotion, and Royce glanced over to see a boy shoved onto the bench behind him—and his heart lifted to see it was Mark. He had made it.

Mark looked back at Royce, equal surprise and gratitude in his eyes.

"You should have let me die," Mark said with a grin, as a soldier roughly handed him an oar. "You saved my life at the expense of your own, and don't think I shall ever forget that. You shall have me at your back, always—assuming we survive."

Mark reached out and Royce clasped his forearm. It felt good to have a friend, to have someone he could trust here.

"And I can say the same of you," Royce replied.

Royce looked out to the sea as they rowed, their ship gaining momentum.

"Where are they taking us?" Royce asked.

"The Red Isle," Mark replied. "From what I hear, it will make our ship ride seem like a fairytale. They say its shore is stained with blood."

Royce felt his apprehension deepen.

"I think the point of this journey is to kill most of us," Mark continued. "And for whoever survives, they will let the isle kill the rest."

Royce wondered as he watched the isle near. It was the most inhospitable place he had ever seen. He saw no signs of life on it, and it certainly seemed like a place to go to die.

Royce went back to rowing, his body shaking from the effort, and as he fell back into the monotony of it, he looked over and noticed the scars across Mark's back from where he had been flogged. He wondered if his back bore the same scars. He arched it, and it still felt raw from where the nobles had beaten him. He noticed a small sun insignia tattooed into the back of Mark's left shoulder, and it made him wonder who he was, and where he was from.

Royce was about to ask him about it, when suddenly three boys sat down on the bench beside him, sliding over and squeezing in beside him—too close. They were broader and larger than him, and he could feel their hot, sweaty bodies beside him.

Royce looked over, surprised, as one removed a dagger and held it up against his throat, the blade hurting. The boy looked furtively around to make sure the guards weren't watching. Royce could barely breathe. He wished he had reacted sooner, but it had all happened too fast.

He smiled a cruel smile, showing yellow teeth. His head was shaved bald, and he had several chins, being overweight. Yet he was also muscular.

"Do you remember me?" he asked. "The name is Rubin. I want to be sure it is one you never forget. These two boys are my friends, Seth and Sylvan. Twins. But you'd never guess by looking at them."

Royce glanced over and saw the two other boys, neither smiling, and neither resembling the other. They both bore dark features, yet one, Seth, was thin, with a lean, angry look, while the other, Sylvan, was muscular, with a broad face and nose, and a neck as large as Royce had ever seen.

Rubin smiled, prodding the knife to Royce's throat.

"Now that we'll all be best friends," he continued, "you can start by handing me that chain of yours."

Royce looked down, and was surprised to see that the necklace Genevieve had given him—the only thing he had ever owned—was now openly on display, the golden wire gleaming in the light. Stupid of him. He had kept it safely hidden all this time, under his shirt; but in the storm his tunic had become frayed.

"Hand it over!" Rubin hissed. "Or the fish will have more food."

Royce wanted to fight back, but the boys were much larger than he was, and had slid all the way over, squeezing him against the hull and leaving him no room to maneuver. He felt the point of the dagger pushed up against his throat, and he did not doubt for a moment that they would kill him.

The thought of handing over the necklace left him with a profound sense of tragedy. The necklace was all he had left of Genevieve, and he held it dear. It was the one thing that had given him hope since he'd boarded the ship.

As the dagger was pushed deeper into Royce's throat, Royce sensed motion from the corner of his eye, and suddenly there came a cracking sound, as Mark spun around and kicked Rubin in his face. Rubin fell backward and dropped the knife.

Royce wasted no time. He lunged forward and tackled Seth and Sylvan at once, driving them backward, tackling them down to the ground and jumping on top of them.

"Fight!" came a chorus of shouts as Royce wrestled with them. Suddenly they were surrounded by boys.

Royce wasted no time. He punched Seth, then wheeled and elbowed Sylvan. Yet as he hit one, the other pounced on top of him, making it impossible for him to gain momentum. Finally, Sylvan rolled on top and grabbed for Royce's face, digging his fingers into his cheeks and trying to gouge out his eyes.

Royce knew that if he did not act fast, he would succeed. He had no other choice: he threw both of his arms in between the boy's wrists, broke his grip, and raised his forehead as his head came down.

There came a crack, and Royce saw he had broken Sylvan's broad nose. Sylvan cried out, clutching it, and rolled off.

No sooner had he done so than Seth jumped atop him.

Royce felt several guards grabbing him, pulling him to his feet, while they pulled Seth off. He was thrown roughly across the deck, back to his seat at the bench, while beside him Mark—who had beaten Rubin back as well—was thrown, too. The two landed beside each other, as the guards drew their swords.

"Back to the oars!" they commanded. "Fight again and you'll all be thrown overboard. We need to lighten this ship anyway!"

"Save your fighting," the other guard added with an evil grin. "Where you're going, you'll need it."

Royce and Mark went back to rowing, and Royce looked over and grinned at Mark.

"It is I who owe you now," Royce said to him.

Mark grinned back.

"No you don't. That was fun," he replied.

Royce and Mark looked at the looming island together. Having Mark beside him, Royce felt a little less alone in this ship full of thieves, bullies, and criminals. He knew he was sailing to his death, but it felt better not doing it alone.

"That isle will kill us both, you know," Mark said.

Royce nodded. He knew it to be true.

"But if we have each other's back," Mark said, "we may live long enough, just long enough, to return back to the mainland, and see the people we love."

Mark held out his forearm, and Royce clasped it.

"You die, I die," Mark said.

Royce nodded. He liked the sound of that.

"You die," he replied, "I die."

CHAPTER THIRTEEN

Royce grabbed hold of the ship's rail as it approached the shore. A moment later it slammed into the rocks and bobbed as the waves pulled it back. It crashed again and again into the craggy boulders that acted as a shoreline for the Red Isle, the boys helpless to steer it.

"Ropes!" the soldiers cried. "Anchors!"

Royce immediately jumped into action, Mark at his side, as they ran with the other boys, grabbed the long, thick ropes coiled on deck, and threw them overboard. The ropes were heavy, wet with sea foam, and coarse, cutting into his palms, which were already calloused from hours of rowing. They stung at the touch.

As Royce tossed the heavy ropes overboard, making sure the line was secure to the mast, his shoulders ached, and he was relieved, at least, that the journey was done. This isle may very well hold death, but at least it would be a death on dry land, and not, like so many boys, on this cursed ship.

Royce heard a commotion and looked out to see the fierce faces of the soldiers waiting to greet them on the rocks below. They grabbed the ropes and secured them, pulling the ship in, and as Royce looked at this welcoming party, he wondered if arriving here was a relief. They were greeted by cold, hard gazes, summing up the new crop of boys. They stood on a beach made of sharp, black rocks, stretching the length of the isle. Fields of black soil lay behind it, no trees in sight. The isle looked completely lifeless, no birds, no animals, no sound other than the crashing of the waves and groaning of their ship.

These warriors were clearly hardened men, overgrown, muscle-bound, heads shaved, faces covered in scars. They wore a black, lightweight mesh armor, furs over their shoulders, gold insignias branded on them. All wore long beards and sour faces, as if they had never learned to smile. Clearly, this was a place of men.

Before them all stood a man who appeared to be their leader, larger than the others, with broad shoulders, extra furs, hard black eyes, and one of his ears mangled. He stood there, hands on his hips while his men worked the ropes, and stared up at the boys in disgust, as if the sea had washed up something foul.

"Welcome to home," Mark muttered sarcastically to Royce under his breath.

"MOVE!" bellowed a voice behind them.

Royce, shoved from behind, fell in line with the other boys, herded toward a wide plank lowered from the ship. Royce watched as the plank fell through the air in an arc thirty feet high, and landed on the rocks below with a bang. Beneath it waves crashed, and sharks, he could see from here, swarmed in the waters. The plank was narrow and crowded.

Royce, prodded from behind, joined the others as they all hiked down the makeshift ramp. It groaned beneath them with the weight of all the boys disembarking at once. Royce understood too well why they were so eager to get off this ship. Yet at the same time, he wondered what the rush was: did they not realize a different death awaited them on this isle?

They stampeded down the plank like an army of elephants, and there soon arose cursing as the boys shoved and elbowed each other. Royce heard one boy cry out and glanced back to see Rubin, the bully who had tried to take his necklace, who had tormented those down below, with his bald head, double chin, narrow brown eyes, and angry jaw, turn and put a shoulder into one boy. The boy shrieked as he fell from the plank, still a good thirty feet up, and into the waters.

Within seconds he was swarmed by the school of sharks, tearing him to pieces as he shrieked. Finally he was dragged under, the waters turning red.

Royce, sickened, looked away. Death, it seemed, awaited them at every turn.

Royce glared back at Rubin, filled with anger and disgust, and Rubin returned the glare.

"What are you looking at?" Rubin barked.

Royce silently vowed to take vengeance for that boy. Rubin's time would come.

They kept moving and Royce continued quickly down the plank, Mark beside him, all the boys pressing in close, not wanting to meet the same fate. Soon Royce stepped foot on a boulder, and he breathed a sigh of relief to feel dry land beneath his feet. He took a few more steps and found himself on a black beach of rocks.

"Line up!" cried the guards.

They all lined up beside each other, and Royce looked over to see that there were only about a hundred survivors left. The numbers stunned him. When they had departed there had been several hundred aboard. Had they lost that many to the sea?

Lined up side by side, they all faced the warrior Royce could only assume to be their new commander, and as Royce looked up into his hardened face, his cold black eyes assessing them as he walked up and down the line, he shivered. This man was formidable, a man to be respected. Towering over all the others, with dark skin, a wide jaw, a bald head, and a scar running from chin to ear, he looked to be afraid of nothing. He was like a walking mountain.

He walked slowly up and down the line, surveying them, and Royce could feel his heart pounding in the silence, the air thick with tension. Without rhyme or reason the commander suddenly walked up to a boy and punched him with an uppercut to his mouth.

The boy fell flat on his back, moaning in pain. He then sat up.

"What did I do?" the boy asked.

The commander grinned.

"You exist," he replied, his voice as deep and hard as his appearance. "And next time, you will address me as Commander Voyt."

Commander Voyt stepped over the boy's head, smiling an evil grin as he continued surveying the others.

"Welcome to the Red Isle," Voyt boomed, his voice ominous and anything but welcoming. "Home for centuries to the best fighters our kingdom has to offer. I am your master. Your owner. You will look up to me as if I am God. Because I *am* God in this place. If I decide you die, you die. If I decide you live, well, you live for now. Until you die at some other time. Do you treasure life that much that you wish to live longer—only to die later?"

It was a curious question, and as he continued to pace the ranks, Royce wasn't certain he was seeking an answer. He seemed to look into each boy's soul as he passed them.

"That is the central question here, one you will learn to ask yourself: how many times will you pray to die? To die the death of training? Training to die in glory."

He paced, hands behind his back, and as he looked out at the sea, he looked as if he were talking more to himself, as if he had seen endless crops of boys arrive and die.

"When you have reached the end of your training—*if* you do," he continued, "you'll be sent to the Pits. There you will learn what true death means. You'll find yourself pitted against savages from every corner of the world. Men who are as likely to bite off your faces as clasp your hand. They show no mercy. They seek no mercy. And that is our motto here on the Red Isle: *Show No Mercy.*

Seek No Mercy. It is one you will learn too well. For that is the way of steel."

He took a deep breath as he continued pacing.

"The Red Isle, *my* isle, turns boys into men. It takes criminals and killers and turns them into warriors; it takes the living and turns them into a walking death. You will be haunted here, and the nightmares will plague you the rest of your life. If you are worthless, as most of you are, you will die. Those of you who are not ready to become men, will die. Those of you who are weak, those of you who are not killers, will die. This is the isle where weakness dies. Where the strong come to flourish."

He stopped in the center, leaned back, and gave a broad smile.

"Welcome, my friends, my servants, my less than nothing scum, to the Red Isle."

Voyt turned abruptly and began to march for the mainland, his soldiers falling in behind him. There came a commotion and as Royce felt himself shoved, he fell in line with the others as they all began to follow.

A horn was sounded from behind Royce, and he turned to see the ship's plank rise, the ropes pulled in, the ship beginning to depart. He felt a pit in his stomach as it began to sail away, out to sea, farther and farther from shore.

Royce turned back and faced the death before him, the black, barren isle, and he sensed that he would never reach home again.

CHAPTER FOURTEEN

Genevieve stood beside the window in the torch-lit chamber and peered down at the castle's courtyard below, no longer trying to stop the tears from running down her cheeks. The rustling continued behind her, and she felt a deepening dread as she knew it was Altfor, slowly getting undressed, removing his wedding finery, one piece at a time. The time had come for them to consummate their marriage.

Genevieve had been led to this chamber earlier in the night, and as she'd walked in she'd been struck by the enormous four-poster bed dominating the room, draped in silks and furs the likes of which she had never dreamed. Luxurious tapestries hung from the walls, silk rugs adorned the stone, and in the corner, a fireplace burned.

None of it held any sway for Genevieve. On the contrary, it felt like a tomb. Filled with dread, she looked up at the stars in the sky and she wished, she prayed with all her heart and soul, that she were anywhere else. She looked out and searched the horizon and wondered about Royce. He was somewhere out there, alive or dead, she did not know. She prayed he would sail back to her, and escape with her this time for good. What she wouldn't give to have her simple life back again.

Genevieve heard Altfor take a step toward her and she snapped out of it, remembering instead the awful image of the day's wedding ceremony. She felt a knot in her stomach at the thought. It had been a formal, royal affair, Genevieve standing there, present in person but not in her soul. She stood numb throughout the entire event, even as Altfor had smiled and kissed her. He had taken her hand and turned and faced the crowd, and the nobles had all nodded back approvingly as the newlyweds walked back down the aisle.

Genevieve closed her eyes and shook her head, trying to wipe it all from her mind. It was the ultimate betrayal to Royce, to the one man she loved in the world. How, she wondered, had she allowed it to come to this?

Her new sister-in-law's words rang in her head.

Become the worm from within. Give them time. Allow them to think you love them. Allow their guard to lower. And then, when they are comfortable, strike.

Moira had a point, of course. The nobles had not been attacked from the outside for centuries. But a foe from the inside, that could topple them. Her marriage, she knew, was the best way to ultimately avenge her people—and free Royce.

She knew it would require patience and cunning, and Genevieve was not good at playing games. She was who she was, and had a hard time pretending to be anyone else.

"My love?"

Genevieve flinched at the sudden voice, shattering the silence, like a knife in her back. She heard Altfor approach a few feet behind, and her heart pounded as she felt his hands on her shoulders. They were gentle hands, yet they felt like icicles on her body.

She did not move to turn, though, and he let out a long sigh.

"I am not like the other lords here, who would take you forcefully," he said softly in her ear. "I will only take you willingly. When you are ready. When you ask me to."

Genevieve was startled by his words. They were words she had never expected a noble to utter.

She turned to face him, and she could see that his face was earnest. It held kindness and compassion, which also surprised her. It was a face starkly unlike his cruel brother's.

"I am not at all like my brother," he continued, surprising her, as if reading her mind. "We share the same parents, but that is all. My brother was an immature, foolhardy man. A violent and willful man. I did not approve of him snatching women from the fields. It is not something I myself have ever done. I loved him in his way—we are brothers after all. But I am not him."

Genevieve took a deep breath, summing him up.

"Yet you have taken me in marriage and away from my people," Genevieve replied coldly. "In a way, that is worse."

"I have taken you not as a plaything, but to marry," he replied. "There is a difference."

She shook her head.

"You are wrong," she replied. "You are the same as your brother. You take me with a ceremony and a smile; he did so with aggression. Either way, I do not wish to be taken."

He stared back, his face dropping, and she could see her words had reached him.

"You are wrong," he replied.

She blinked back.

"So then I am free to leave?" she asked.

"No," he replied, his voice hard. "You are not free to leave. You are mine now. You belong to me, to this family. You will bear me sons. Perhaps daughters, too. But I won't force you. I will give you time. You will learn to love me."

Genevieve felt a sense of disgust welling within her, along with a stubborn determination to never love him. She frowned, feeling her anger, her hopelessness, course through her. She realized even in her anger how different Altfor was than the other nobles and perhaps it was his nobility, his lack of cruelty, that inflamed her. It would have been easier if he were violent and cruel like the others.

"I shall *never* learn to love you," she insisted. "My heart lies with another. And as long as I am alive, until I die with my last breath, I shall always love him. You may have me; yet you have but a shell of me. He has my entire heart, and he shall have it forever."

She expected Altfor to be angry; she *wanted* him to be angry.

Yet to her great surprise and disappointment, he merely smiled back and caressed her cheek with the back of his gentle hand.

"I will leave you now," he replied. "We will sleep in separate chambers. But one day you shall seek me out." He smiled, caressing her cheek. "Love," he concluded, "you will find can have many different meanings."

CHAPTER FIFTEEN

Royce marched in a long row of boys, his legs aching, slipping on the wet rocks that made up this isle, and wondering, as the sun hung low in the gray sky, if this trek would ever end. They crested yet another hill and he looked out, hopeful that this time a destination would lie before them.

His heart fell in disappointment. There, as far as the eye could see, was more of the same: an endless wasteland, no landmarks in sight, the ground composed of slick, black rock interlaced with small puddles, stretching for an eternity. His stomach grumbled, weak from hunger. They'd had no break, no water, no food. Worst of all, the incessant, biting wind would not leave them be. His clothes were still wet from the voyage, and were too light, besides, for the weather here. The dampness made his clothes stick to his skin, and the cold sank deep into his bones. He looked at the other boys and saw he was not the only one shivering, and he found himself looking at his captors' furs and envying them more than ever. The soldiers here were all heavily dressed, bedecked in furs, shielding the cold, with thick boots that could handle the slippery, rocky terrain—unlike all the new arrivals, including himself, who were badly equipped for this clime, terrain, or march. It was all a test, Royce realized.

They paused atop the hill, and Voyt turned and faced the boys, wearing a satisfied smirk.

"I know you all are cold. And tired. And hungry. Very good," he said with a smile. "Feel what it feels like to suffer. Embrace it. It is the only friend you will have here."

He breathed, hands on hips, and Royce could tell he relished the bleakness of this place.

"Turn around and face the sea," he commanded.

Royce turned with the others and peered into the distance. It was gray and thick with fog, and he could barely even see a glimmer of the horizon.

"Behind you there lies nothing," Voyt continued. "Before you lies nothing. Except the faintest glimmer of hope. Before that, you will march. A march that will take you to the end of all that you are. This is how we welcome initiates here. It is the march of the worthy."

He surveyed them all as the wind howled amidst the silence.

"Only the worthy will survive this march," he continued. "Many have taken it before you, and many have died on this very stone. Feel free to lie down and give up any time. Most do. You will spare me the effort of killing you later."

There came a noise and Royce turned to see one of the boys, a tall, skinny lad who had seemed to barely cling to life throughout the journey, step out of line, drop to his knees, and clasp his hands together, begging for mercy.

"Please," he called out, weeping. "I can't take another step. I'm too cold," he said, his teeth chattering. "Too tired. Too weak. I cannot go on. Please. Let us rest. Mercy!"

All the boys watched nervously as Voyt walked slowly over to the boy, his boots crunching on the gravel. He suddenly drew his sword and, before Royce could even process what was happening, stabbed the boy in the heart.

The boy gasped and dropped onto his side, unmoving, eyes open. Dead.

Royce looked down at him, stunned.

"There is mercy," Voyt said, calmly, to the dead body.

Voyt turned and looked out at the group of boys.

"Does anyone else wish for mercy?" he asked.

Royce stood there, heart pounding, and none of the boys moved.

Finally, slowly, Voyt turned and continued to march, back into the bleakness.

*

Royce marched and marched, one foot at a time, and was surprised to find himself slipping in something soft. He looked down and realized the terrain had changed from black rock to black mud as they began to descend a new hill. Mark, beside him, lost his balance and began to fall, and Royce reached out and grabbed his arm, steadying him.

Mark gave him a look of gratitude as they continued to walk side-by-side.

"I don't think I can make it," Mark finally confided.

Royce noticed how pale his friend looked, how unsteady on his feet, and he worried for him.

"You *will* make it," Royce said. Royce had been feeling on the verge of dying himself, but at his new friend's words, he felt a sudden surge of strength. He realized that when he took his mind off of himself and put it on other woes, when he focused on worrying for others and not for himself, all his weariness went away.

"You *must* make it," Royce continued. "*We* must make it. You made a vow, remember? To watch my back. And I yours. You can't watch it if you're dead."

Mark looked back and grinned, and he seemed to gain a bounce to his step.

"I remember," he conceded. "For you, I will do it. But once we arrive to camp—I will die. Then you shall watch your own back."

Royce laughed.

"Deal," he agreed.

Suddenly, Royce felt himself shoved from behind and he stumbled, losing his balance, and fell to the mud. He felt a pain in his hand and looked down to see he had scraped his palms on a sharp rock.

Furious, Royce stood and turned, looking for the culprit. Behind him he saw Rubin, smiling back, flanked by Seth and Sylvan. They all laughed at Royce.

"Maybe you'll watch where you're going next time," Rubin mocked.

Royce felt a wave of fury. He sensed right away that this boy was a bully, a predator, testing everyone, looking for the weak ones he could dominate. Royce had seen him do it to others on the ship, testing them as far as they could go until he finally broke them— and eventually killing them. Royce knew he was being singled out now, that he was being tested. He could not allow it to happen.

Seeing red, Royce charged. He came close and kicked, sweeping his legs around, kicking Rubin as hard as he could and aiming for the back of his knees. He connected with the soft flesh behind his knee, and as he did, he kicked Rubin's legs out from under him and sent him flying, till he landed flat on his back.

The boys crowded around, instantly cheering.

"FIGHT!"

Royce pounced before Rubin could get up, kneeling atop him, grabbing his neck and squeezing.

Rubin, though, was surprisingly strong. He grabbed at Royce's hand, pulling it off, yet Royce held on, determined, as if it were a matter of life and death.

"Test me," Royce seethed, "and I will kill you. I've nothing left to lose. Try me."

Royce knew he should stop, yet he kept squeezing. He squeezed until the boy's face turned purple. Royce was overcome with rage. He couldn't take it anymore. He was in a rage at being taken away from Genevieve, from his brothers, from everyone he loved in the world. He could not tolerate any more meanness.

Out of the corner of his eye Royce saw the twins coming for him. He saw Mark rushing forward and tackling them, sending them both to the ground.

Suddenly, Royce felt himself kicked in the chest by a huge boot and he was airborne, flying off the boy; he tumbled on the rock, and then was kicked across the face.

Royce, in pain, rolled and groaned and looked up. Voyt stood over him, while another soldier stood over Mark, kicking him off the twins and separating them.

Voyt sneered.

"*I'll* tell you when it's time to kill," he admonished Royce. "Until then, be grateful I don't kill you myself."

Royce stood and looked over to see Mark, wiping blood from his lip, too. Rubin and the twins slowly stood, scowling back at Royce and Mark. But this time they did not laugh or attempt to approach him. He had stood up to the bully and had proven his point.

"You and me," Rubin said, pointing threateningly at him. "Later."

Royce opened his arms wide.

"Come now," he said, not backing down.

But Rubin turned, grinning, and strutted off with the twins. But this time, Royce noticed, they kept their distance.

Rubin acted as if he had won, and yet Royce knew he had gained his respect. And not just his. Royce glanced around and saw the faces of dozens of other boys, potential enemies, potential friends, staring at him. They learned, too. He would not lie down.

That was valuable, Royce knew.

In a place like this, that was more valuable than gold.

*

The sky had turned dark by the time Royce, frozen to the bone, weary with exhaustion, weak with hunger, stepped onto real grass. He looked down at first, puzzled, not understanding why the texture had changed beneath his feet. He had been lost in a world of fantasy, had been imagining himself anywhere but here. He had seen himself back at home, with his brothers, reaping the fall harvest, so happy to be alive. He had seen himself reunited with Genevieve, on their wedding day, about to exchange vows.

But now, as he stepped onto the soft new surface, he looked up for the first time in hours and saw the night sky. It wasn't quite black in this part of the world, but streaked with phosphorescent purples and greens. He had lost count of how many hours—or was it days and nights?—they had been marching. He looked behind him and saw that of the hundred boys who had come off the ship and set out on this trek, only a few dozen now remained. The others had died somewhere along the way, dropping on the isle like flies, landing on the stone with no one to bury them. The birds that increasingly followed them, though, huge vulture-like things, hardly waited before descending on their corpses.

Royce, teeth chattering, looked over and was relieved to see his friend Mark still alive beside him, though he was hunched over now, barely able to walk. He glanced back over his other shoulder and was disappointed to see Rubin was still alive, the twins, too, all glaring back with hatred as if they'd been staring the entire time. Hatred, Royce realized, could outlive anything.

Royce looked out before him and was surprised to find, on the far end of the grassy field, a structure, the first he had seen in this entire isle. It appeared to be a large cave carved into the side of a mountain—and inside the cave, Royce was shocked to see, raged a roaring bonfire. Around its flames there glowed the faces of what appeared to be a hundred soldiers, all standing there, waiting.

Royce, with a rush of hope, suddenly understood what this meant. He had done it. He had survived the march of the worthy.

Even better, Royce was suddenly struck by the smell of roasting meat. It hit him in the stomach. On the fire he spotted small, roasting game, along with jugs of water, and of wine. He never thought he would smell food again. Would they allow him? he suddenly wondered with panic. Or was this all a cruel trick?

Voyt stopped before them all, turned, and smiled.

"Tonight," he boomed, his voice dark, commanding and oddly as full of energy as when Royce had first heard it, as if the trek across the world had not fazed him at all, "you dine with men. You enjoy the warmth of the fire. The water. The wine. You few who have survived have earned it."

He took a deep breath.

"And tomorrow," he added, "you shall learn what it means to become men. Rest up, for this may be the last night that many of you shall have on this earth."

Royce stood there, cold and exhausted and hungry, barely able to even move, and watched as the other soldiers slowly left the fire and walked out to embrace their fellow soldiers. The dozen surviving boys headed toward the fire like moths to a flame, and Royce walked with them, grabbing Mark's arm and prodding him along.

Soon they reached the bonfire, and Royce held out his shaking hands before it. Slowly, the pain struck him, a million needles in his fingers, his hands coming back to life. He rubbed them, slowly at first, awkwardly, and they began to thaw. It was painful; but it was exquisite.

Royce reached out to Mark, still hunched over, and helped him hold up his hands. He then went over to one of the roasting spits of meat, and looked up at the soldiers standing nearby. They nodded back down, granting permission.

Royce took two pieces and gave one to Mark first.

"Eat," he urged.

Mark reached up, took the piece, and slowly took a bite.

Royce took a bite himself, and it was the best feeling of his life. He chewed and took bite after bite, barely swallowing before chewing more.

Royce felt something heavy on his shoulders, and looked back to see a soldier had draped a heavy fur over him. The soldiers were going from boy to boy, draping a thick, heavy fur over each. Royce realized it was a badge of honor, a gift for the survivors. He wrapped the fur tight over his shoulders, and for the first time since arriving here he felt impervious to the winds of the isle.

Royce took the jug of wine that the soldiers were passing around, took a long sip, and immediately felt the warmth spreading through his body. This, combined with the furs and the warmth of the fire, slowly brought him back to life.

Tomorrow, he might die. But tonight, and for this moment, he was alive again.

CHAPTER SIXTEEN

Royce was awakened by rough hands on his back, yanking him to his feet. He stood there, wobbly, still in the world of dreams and unsure if he was awake or asleep. Disoriented, he opened his eyes, on alert, wondering what was happening. He looked out and saw the world was scarlet, the breaking dawn before him seeming to fill the entire world, and he had never felt more exhausted in his life. He felt as if he had just closed his eyes to sleep a moment ago. Still knocked out from the march, it had been the deepest—and shortest—sleep of his life.

Royce heard a commotion and saw all the other boys being jerked to their feet, too, all roughly rounded up by the soldiers. The smell of smoke heavy in the air, he looked over and saw the bonfire was smoldering, and he realized, in his exhaustion, he had collapsed beside it the night before. His clothes reeked of smoke.

At least now, though, his body felt warm. Yesterday he had been as cold as he had ever been, certain he would never get warm again. Now, with the thick furs, the warm food and wine in his belly and the night he had spent beside the flames, he felt ready to face the world again.

"Move out!" a voice yelled, piercing the morning silence.

Royce saw Mark standing beside him, looking half-dead, but before he had a chance to speak to him he suddenly felt a sharp pain in his back, jolting him fully awake. He spun to see he been jabbed in the small of his back by a long staff, a soldier scowling back as he moved up and down the line, jabbing all the boys, herding them like sheep.

Royce moved with all the others down a hill of rock and soon found himself standing in a field of mud. He and the boys lined up beside each other, all surrounded by the soldiers, who formed a broad, wide circle. Royce, heart pounding, wondered what was happening. He didn't like the looks of it.

Long, wooden staffs suddenly flew through the air as soldiers each threw one toward the boys. One was aimed right for him, and Royce snatched it midair, wondering.

Voyt stepped forward sternly and addressed them.

"A few dozen of you against a hundred of us," he said, grinning. "You will learn to fight together, and to fight as a team.

You will learn to need each other. In the Pits you will fight alone. But in order to learn how to fight for oneself, one must first learn how to fight for others."

A horn sounded, there came a great shout, and suddenly the dozens of soldiers charged. Royce braced himself as the soldiers bore down with heavy, wooden swords, raising them high for maximum damage.

Without thinking, Royce raised his staff to block. The soldier came down with such strength that Royce thought it would snap his staff in two. The staff held. Yet the vibration ran through Royce's arms, his attacker's strength surprising him.

The clacking of wood filled the air, as Royce blocked one blow after the next, the soldier driving him back. He raised his staff and stopped a sword slash before it came down for his head, then sidestepped and blocked another blow before it reached his ribs. He saw an opening and lowered his staff and then brought it up high, knocking the sword from his attacker's hands. He was stunned he had done so, and pleased with himself.

But he then felt a terrible pain in his back, and he dropped to a knee and turned to see he had been whacked by another soldier, in his kidney. The pain was unbearable.

Before he could gather himself, he suddenly felt an awful pain in his head, as he was whacked yet again.

He dropped face-first onto the mud, feeling a lump forming on his head.

"Get up!" a soldier snarled, standing over him. "Warriors don't quit."

He shoved Royce with his boot, rolling him over in the mud, and as Royce looked up, he saw the wooden sword coming down for his chest. He knew it would really hurt, and that he didn't have much time.

Royce suddenly realized if he wanted to survive this place, he would have to rise above his pain, above his suffering. He would have to learn to survive—and even thrive—while in the midst of pain.

Royce, determined, forced himself to fight back. He felt a sudden rush of rage, a determination not to get beaten down here in the mud, however imposing the foe, and as the sword came down, he rolled, swung around with his staff, and whacked the soldier hard behind the knees. The blow knocked the soldier off his feet, and Royce watched with satisfaction as the man fell to his back.

Royce jumped to his feet, spun, and blocked the blow from another soldier, right before it hit his face. He stepped forward and jabbed his staff into the other attacker's solar plexus, dropping him, with a whoomph, to his knees.

Royce, invigorated, spun every way, fighting for his life, fully awake, determined not to go down again. He was reeling from the pain and bumps and bruises, but was determined to rise above it. Holding his staff with two hands, he blocked a mighty blow of the sword as it came down right for his head. He then leaned back and kicked his attacker, driving him back.

Another soldier rushed him from the side, and this time, Royce was able to detect him. He did not know how, but as he fought, it was as if his abilities were fine tuning, as if some foreign force were overtaking him. He reached around and jabbed the man with his staff before he could get close.

He then spun and whacked another soldier across the hands as he lowered his sword, disarming him.

He then ducked as a blow came for his head, swung around, and cracked another attacker in the back.

Royce fought like a man possessed. He felt a familiar energy rising within him, one he had never understood but was learning to embrace. It spread throughout his chest, his palms, a warmth, a surge. He looked around and the world slowed and came into focus. He could see everything in minute detail. The sounds became muted, and it was as if, for just a moment, the universe existed solely for him.

Royce saw the other boys getting beaten, falling in all directions. Some dropped to their knees as they were slashed and jabbed in the stomach; others were struck across the back. Even Rubin and the twins were on the ground, on their bellies in the mud, staffs long knocked from their hands, as soldiers whacked them again and again. Blows rained down upon them from all directions. It was a beating. A trial by fire. This was no sparring match.

It was a brutal initiation.

He realized with a sudden fury that some of these boys might even die from these blows.

Royce was filled with indignation. It was unfair. This entire isle, his entire reason for being sent here, was unfair. He railed at the injustice of the universe. They weren't looking to train them, he suddenly realized. They were looking to break them.

Royce refused to let himself die. Not this way.

Royce felt something course through him then—strength, rage, certainty. His body knew what to do even if he didn't. Here, in this desolate place, at the end of the earth, with nothing left to lose, the power came to him. Royce allowed himself to be subsumed by it.

He allowed himself, for the first time, to be controlled by something he did not understand.

Suddenly, the world came rushing back to full speed again. He swung his staff with all his might, knocking the sword from an approaching soldier's hands. The soldier, much larger, looked at him, stunned, and Royce brought his staff straight up, connecting under his chin and knocking him flat on his back.

Royce ducked a blow and lifted up, using his back to send a soldier flying. He then spun, again and again, cutting through the crowd, attacking instead of retreating. He was like a fox, darting in and out of them, spinning and striking, ducking and jabbing, leaving a field of victims in his wake. No one could touch him.

Royce moved like a snake through water. He did not allow himself to stop even for a moment, and soon, he was dimly aware that he was downing all of the soldiers in the field.

As the rage consumed him, Royce felt caught up in a blur of motion, swinging and striking, kicking, jumping, throwing himself into the battle with careless abandon. He felt himself melting into the power of the universe. And for the first time in his life, he felt invincible.

When it was all done, Royce hardly knew what had happened. He stood there, breathing hard, and took in the now-quiet scene, shocked. Lying on the ground around him were nearly a hundred men, soldiers, all on their hands and knees, all in a state of shock.

But what unnerved Royce most was the look they all gave him. It was not only shock. Not only awe.

They looked at him as if he were different.

And he felt it himself, coursing in his veins. He was not of these boys, of these men.

He *was* different.

But how?

Who, after all, was he?

CHAPTER SEVENTEEN

Dust sat in silence as the sailors rowed a small boat in toward the kingdom's shore. The sailors stared at him in obvious horror and dislike, and Dust couldn't decide if it was because they had never seen a gray-skinned man before, because the gray silks of the dead unnerved them, or because they recognized the tattoos that traced across his face.

He sat waiting, watching the flight of the sea birds and reading the signs to be found in them. There were signs in most things, from the ways flames danced above a fire, to the spill of guts in a sacrificed goat. Dust might not have the great magic found amongst the priests or the magicians, but he knew these things, and many others.

He knew, for example, that the sailors planned to betray him. It was not a thought that filled him with any particular fear, although there were three of them and Dust carried no obvious weapon, no sword or spear. It brought with it at best a kind of mild irritation that people could be so foolish. They must know what he was, so why risk it?

"We're here," one of the sailors said, as if Dust could not feel the scrape of the boat against the sand for himself.

He hopped out, and so did the sailors. Idly, Dust wondered how they planned to do this. Perhaps they would teach him something new. Then again, probably not. Men such as this had so little experience with the true ways of death. They started to spread out around him, forming a rough triangle.

"We swore to your lot that we'd carry you safe to shore," one of the men said. "We didn't say anything about what would happen after."

Dust ignored that. "When I was a boy, men came to my door and killed my entire family. They did this because the magi of my order had observed certain signs. They took me into their home, and they raised me."

"Think we want your life story right when we're going to kill you?" another of the sailors asked.

"Think hearing how pampered you were is going to stop us?"

"Pampered?" Dust said with a smile. "Every day, I was beaten. I was accustomed to pain. I saw things die in front of me. I was made to train until my hands bled, and learn until my mind hurt with it. They took me and they molded me into an *angarim*. Do you know what that means?"

"Don't know, don't care," the last of the men said, lunging at Dust's back, as Dust had known he would. When it came to the ways of death, most people were so predictable.

He turned, swaying aside from the attack, his foot coming down with a crunch on the man's knee. As his attacker's leg collapsed, he was already moving, stepping inside the arc of a hatchet and driving stiffened fingers into the throat of a second attacker. His hands went up to the man's skull as he gagged and Dust wrenched sideways at the perfect angle, hearing the snap of a breaking neck.

The last man came at him and Dust dropped under the sweep of a broadsword, his hand coming up with a rock as he rolled. He spun and threw it at the first man who had attacked him, seeing it collide with the temple; another of the spots where death might enter.

The last man stood there staring. "What are you?"

"As I told you, I am *angarim*. In your tongue, I believe it might translate as 'one with death.' I understand it. I serve it. I was trained to bring it where it is required, through every means, fast and slow." Dust reached into his sleeves, drawing out a pair of long, dagger-like needles. "In your case, I think I will make it slow."

His opponent started forward, but Dust was already in motion, throwing first one needle, then the next. They struck where he intended; how could they not? The man fell to his knees, arms no longer working now that the needles stuck perfectly in the nerve bundles of both shoulders.

Dust drew a small, sharp-bladed knife. "It seems to be the way of things, though, that fools will always find a way to set themselves in the path of what must be done. Now, shall we begin?"

The fool screamed, of course, but that didn't bother Dust. *His* entrails said nothing interesting, but there would be other signs. There always were.

None of it mattered.

There was only one person he truly had to kill, a young man whose existence threatened far too much.

Royce.

And he would stop at nothing until he found him.

CHAPTER EIGHTEEN

Royce stared at the rocky pass that stood in front of him and the other recruits; he was sure that nothing good would come of it, especially with the men he could see standing on either side with spears and bows.

Commander Voyt stood there, gesturing toward it as if welcoming to some grand ball.

"A warrior must be fast and agile as well as strong. He must be able to face danger with all the speed needed to overcome it, but not so much that he becomes reckless and leaves himself open to death. Thus you will run through the canyon, where there are obstacles that could kill you, and men who will throw spears down at you."

Royce swallowed at the sight of it. Even from there, he could see the shine on the spears. They would be sharp.

Commander Voyt wasn't done though. "A cautious man could sneak through, given enough time, but you do not *have* time." He took out a large sand timer and turned it. "The slowest boy through the valley will be killed. Any boy who does not make it through before the sand runs out will be killed. What are you waiting for? An invitation? *Run.*"

Royce ran forward, all the boys jostling and fighting for position. He saw one of the boys stumble and helped him up.

"You shouldn't help anyone. If someone falls, you know that they will be last," the boy said.

Royce shook his head. He couldn't do that to win, even if it put him at greater risk. He would do this fairly, through his own speed and strength.

He set off running, and he could see Mark ahead, pushed here and there by Rufus and the others.

He could see a spearman lining up a throw toward him, too, and ran forward, pushing Mark just as the man released his weapon. It clattered to one side.

"Maybe you should spend less time pushing the others and more time running," Royce suggested, as he and Mark pulled clear of the others.

"You don't need to run with me," Mark said. "I've seen how fast you are; I'd only slow you down."

"If you die, I die," Royce said, reminding his friend of their pact. He ran forward, making sure Mark was with him.

More spears came from above. Royce dodged, finding that it was easy enough to guess their path if he concentrated. He understood the violence of it, and it was easy to slip into the spaces between the weapons. Not every boy was so lucky. Royce saw one pierced through by a weapon, another brought down by an arrow that came from ahead.

There were boulders along the floor of the valley now, and Royce could see boys darting their way from one to another, trying to avoid the arrows coming their way. It looked like a slow process though, and in his mind's eye, Royce could imagine the sand in the timer, slowly trickling away. There didn't seem to be enough time to take things that slowly.

"Trust me," he called back to Mark, and charged forward.

Judging where the arrows were going to come was harder than for the spears. They came faster, and with less wind up from those targeting them. Even so, Royce could do it if he concentrated, guessing the moments when he had to dive for cover behind the rocks, moving quickly from one spot to another.

Soon, they turned another twist in the canyon, and now Royce could see obstacles set up in their path, from walls set with spikes to pits with flames at the bottom and wires set in tangles along the path they were to run.

"Why do all this?" Royce wondered aloud. "Why put us through all this if we're just going to go to the Pits to die anyway?"

It seemed a disgusting thought, to take them all there and work them almost to death just so that they could have a more entertaining death later on. Right then, though, there was no time to think about it; there was only the route in front of them.

"Ready?" Royce asked. As soon as Mark nodded, they started forward. One of the spiked walls was first. Royce might have tried to leap it if he'd been alone, and would probably have ended up impaled on the spikes. Instead, he lifted Mark up, and Mark crouched on the wall, helping Royce to the top in turn. They leapt down to the other side, ready for the flaming pits.

Royce knew there had to be some kind of trick to it. The pits were too wide to jump, so there had to be another way. Then he saw sheets of thick, waterlogged hide nearby. A boy would have to be brave to trust in them, but also smart enough not to try to jump without them. Tossing one to Mark, he took one for himself.

He took a run at the pit, and it flared up as he approached, but he leapt anyway, feeling his feet crunch into the dirt on the other side. He saw Mark land beside him, scrambling for balance. Royce reached out to grab him, pulling him forward.

On the other side, Royce saw a boy copying what they'd done, wrapping himself in one of the hides. Rubin grabbed it from him, pushing the boy away. The boy teetered on the edge of the pit for a moment, and then fell, screaming, the sounds of his death too horrifying to comprehend. Royce could only pull himself away from it because he knew that there was nothing he could do, and the sand timer was still running.

That just left the wires, and Royce wasn't sure how much time they had left to get through them. He tried to chart a route, picking his way through it a step at a time.

Elsewhere, he could see boys dying in them. They snagged wires and spikes shot into them, or blades slashed across to slice at them. One even released a viper from a cage to strike.

Royce knew he couldn't risk touching a single wire. He stared at them, trying to understand. He thought he could see the pattern then. Whoever had laid this out had done so with a definite design in mind, and Royce could see the gaps in that layout.

"This way," he said, stepping from one gap to the next, moving smoothly and quickly. He led the way through, and Mark followed in his wake.

Beyond the wires, they stumbled to the exit to the valley. Commander Voyt was standing there waiting for them, having somehow gotten ahead of them.

"Wait there," he commanded, pointing.

Royce did as he was instructed, and slowly, more and more of the boys started to stumble from the valley, until it seemed that most of those who were going to make it through the traps had done so. Commander Voyt stood there, staring at the sand timer, waiting until every grain of it ran out. Royce could see boys still running along the path to the exit.

Commander Voyt lowered his hand, and the soldiers of the Red Isle moved up to the exit to the canyon, swords at the ready. They didn't hesitate as more boys poured out of the valley, but cut at head height, hacking through necks and sending bodies tumbling to the floor. Royce recognized boys from the boat who had seemed kind, who might have become friends given time. A part of Royce wanted to step forward and try to stop the carnage, but Mark put a hand on his arm.

"There's nothing we can do," his friend whispered.

Commander Voyt turned to them. " Some of you made it. I'm surprised. I was hoping none of you would."

Royce pondered his words, wondering if they were true.

97

CHAPTER NINETEEN

Genevieve sat in her rooms, trying to work out what exactly it was that the wife of a nobleman was meant to do. In one sense, she already knew: she was meant to bear him sons, and that was truly her only function in life. She couldn't bring herself to do it though, not with Altfor, and not when Royce was still out there somewhere.

"I thought I would find you here," Moira said, her sister-in-law coming in without waiting to be asked. Not that Genevieve cared about that kind of thing normally, but here, it felt like the world saying that even this room, even this small scrap of space, was not truly hers.

"Where else would I go?" Genevieve said, not trying to hide her unhappiness.

"You can't let Altfor think that you even *want* to go," Moira said, shaking her head. She went over to the dressing table and poured a goblet of wine from a ewer. "Here, drink this."

Genevieve took it and sipped it, but didn't drink it all even when Moira took wine for herself, drinking more.

"Sensible, not drinking too much," Moira said. "You have to remember that from now on, everything you do and say and are will be judged, if not by Altfor, then by his friends, or by the peasantry."

"I'm *one* of the peasants," Genevieve pointed out.

"You were," Moira shot back, "but the moment you married the Duke, you became more than that. No one you used to know will see you the same way."

"My family would," Genevieve insisted. "I still have parents, and sisters. Sheila would not see me as the wife of a duke."

"No," Moira said. "She would be jealous that she did not have the chance at this position, or grateful that it was not her, or afraid that if you came to her it would put her in danger."

Genevieve shook her head. "You don't know anything about Sheila. You don't know how she would react."

Moira moved to sit on a chair at the side of the room. "Then tell me."

Genevieve hesitated, and then went to sit with her. "You're just looking to make fun of me."

"Hardly that," Moira said. "I know what it's like to be stuck here with little enough to do. Ned spends half his time hunting, and the other half trying to persuade the temples to declare him favored by God. That leaves me here with music, embroidery, the game of courtly seduction…"

"Moira!" Genevieve said, surprised that her sister-in-law would even joke about it.

"Worried about being beheaded for saying the wrong thing?" Moira said. She smiled. "Then tell me all about your family, and save us both."

"I don't know what to say," Genevieve said. "We live… lived, quite simply. Sheila is my oldest sister, and I always thought that she was the pretty one. My parents were always there when I needed anything, even if we didn't have much to share between us."

"It sounds as though you had a beautiful life there," Moira said. "You need to think of that life whenever things get difficult here. You need to draw strength from it."

Genevieve knew that the other woman knew what she was talking about, yet the only thing she could draw strength from right then was the thought of the end of this, either with Altfor's death, or with hers. Whatever it took, she would do it. She didn't care if it led to her downfall, just so long as it meant that the nobleman couldn't get what he wanted from her. She might be his wife, but she would never be his.

Even if it killed her.

Six moons later

CHAPTER TWENTY

Royce lunged, slashing at his friend Mark, the click-clack of wooden swords filling the air as they drove each other back and forth across the summer fields. Royce could not help but notice that they were both stronger now, faster, more hardened—and better warriors. Neither was able to get the best of one another.

They swung and parried like a well-oiled machine, testing and prodding each other's weaknesses, getting better with each swing, as they had for the past six moons. They had trained so much, it was like they could read other's thoughts, and as Royce lunged, again and again, Mark always anticipated, blocking or dodging just in time. Yet Mark, too, could not gain a move on him.

Royce heard the shouts and cheers all around him, dimly aware of the dozen boys surrounding them, egging them on. But six moons ago there were dozens of these boys. But these past six moons had been too cruel, had narrowed their ranks too thinly. There had been losses from starvation, from the bitter cold, from sparring, drowning, encounters with beasts, battles with authority, and from relentless training sessions that were so grueling that some of the boys had dropped dead on the spot.

As Voyt had warned, the weak were weeded out here, day after day.

As Royce slashed, he tried to push from his mind the most recent funeral for one of his brothers-in-arms, earlier this morning, a grim affair for a boy who had drowned while trying to swim across the Great Channel. It had been the final leg of a day-long training session, and as he'd cried for help, caught up in the tides, but feet from shore, no soldiers had gone for him. Nor had they allowed Royce or the others to go for him. It was part of the training, they'd said.

Royce tried to shake the thought from his mind, but the boy's cries still echoed in his head.

Distracted, Royce felt a sting of pain as he suddenly looked up to see Mark landing a blow on his arm. Before he could react, Mark spun his sword around quickly and disarmed him, knocking Royce's sword out of his hand, leaving him defenseless.

Surprised, Royce charged and tackled his friend to the ground, driving him down. The two wrestled on the ground, until Royce managed to get Mark in a lock, grabbing his shoulders and pinning him down.

"Give!" Royce demanded.

"Never!" Mark said.

Mark rolled and threw Royce off of him. The boys cheered as the two of them regained their feet and their swords, facing each other, looking for an opening to lunge again.

"Match!" cried a voice.

Royce and Mark looked over as Voyt marched up and appeared before them, a wooden sword in hand. He scowled down.

"You both fought miserably," he said. "Keep fighting like that, and you shall surely be killed in the Pits."

Royce was unsurprised by his words. Voyt had not had a kind word to say since the day they'd arrived. Yet deep down, secretly, Royce knew that he had improved—very much improved—and he sensed Voyt admired him.

A horn sounded, shouts rang out, and more boys entered the ring and began fighting. The click-clack that never ended on this isle rose again.

On and on it went, as it had hour after hour, day after day.

"Royce!" shouted a voice.

Royce turned to see Voyt scowling down at him, hands on his hips.

"Come with me."

Royce exchanged a glance with Mark, who looked back nervously. Voyt had never summoned any of them before. Royce did not see how this could go well.

Royce turned and followed as all the other boys stared, clearly wondering what this could be about, and he hurried to catch up to Voyt.

"You lose, time and again, because of the way you hold your sword, the way you hold your body," Voyt said, disappointment in his voice, looking ahead as he walked.

Royce frowned.

"I did not lose," he said. "It was a draw."

Voyt huffed.

"A draw is a loss," he chided. "Not winning is a loss. In the Pits, if you don't win, you are dead."

They walked on in silence, up and down rolling hills, Royce's apprehension deepening. None of this boded well. Would he be killed?

Finally, they reached a large, burnt tree, its twisted branches reaching to the sky, and Voyt came to a stop in the clearing beneath it.

Voyt turned and faced him. He drew two real swords from his belt, holding one and throwing the other to Royce.

Royce caught it midair, surprised by the weight of it. He held it up, admiring its heavy metal hilt, the double thick blade. He looked up and saw Voyt grinning, his sword gleaming in the light, and he felt a wave of fear. It was the first time they'd held real swords.

"Have I done something wrong?" Royce asked. "Are you going to kill me?"

Voyt smiled, and Royce realized he had never seen him smile. It came out more like a frown. He was a large, intimidating figure, casting a broad shadow over the entire group, soldiers and boys alike.

"If you are not fast enough, I just might."

Voyt suddenly charged, raising his sword, coming for him. Royce, out of sheer instinct, raised his own sword at the last second and blocked the heavy blow. The sharp clang of metal rang out, and sparks came showering down all around them. The vibration of the blow rang up Royce's arm, through his elbow. He was stunned by the commander's overpowering strength and speed, and he had no idea how he could fight him.

Voyt didn't even pause; he spun his sword around, and in one quick motion slashed Royce's sword. There came the sound of steel scraping steel as he knocked Royce's sword from his hand.

Royce, helpless, watched it go flying, until finally it landed in the dirt several feet away. Voyt held the point of his sword to Royce's neck, and Royce stood there, defenseless, ashamed.

"You are going to have to do a lot better than that," Voyt reprimanded. "Have the past six moons taught you nothing?"

Royce looked down, shamed, feeling the blood rush to his cheeks.

"Why have you brought me here?" Royce asked.

A heavy silence fell as Voyt stepped forward, boots crunching in the gravel. Royce braced himself for a fatal blow.

"To teach you how to stay alive," he replied in his deep voice.

Royce looked up, stunned. He suddenly realized that he wasn't led here to be killed; on the contrary, he realized that Voyt had taken an interest in him. He wondered why.

"Why me?" Royce asked. "Why now?"

Voyt lowered his sword.

"You have a quality unlike the others," Voyt said. "You have a natural feel for war. You see the gaps in a foe's defenses, and you are already moving when the enemy strikes at you. I may be interested to see you live a little bit longer. Then again, I may not. Now go get your sword and stop asking questions."

Royce bolted off after his sword and held it up again. This time he tightened his grip, vowing not to lose it.

Voyt attacked again, groaning as he came down, and Royce blocked it, sparks showering.

"Two hands!" Voyt yelled. "A man holds a sword in one hand when he has something useful to do with the other. If you have a shield, a knife or a cloak, that is the time for one hand. Otherwise, use all your strength!"

Royce tightened his grip as Voyt swung around, a mighty blow that would have chopped a tree in half. Royce deflected the blow in a shower of sparks, his entire body teetering from it.

"You must learn the lessons of a warrior. Use your foe's strengths as weaknesses. Use size against them. Use their lack of speed. Wherever they think they are most dangerous, there is a crack, too. Don't hesitate."

Voyt charged, swinging again and again, side to side, driving Royce back across the clearing beneath the twisted tree. Yet each time, Royce managed to block, drenched in sweat, arms shaking, but surviving. Sparks rained down all over him, Royce barely able to hold his own against Voyt's herculean strength.

"You are slow," Voyt called out as he swung. "Like a duck wading through mud. Because you move with your arms, not with your hips, as you should. Power starts at your feet, not your shoulders. Fight with your feet—and the rest will follow."

Before Royce could process his words, Voyt suddenly swung around with his foot and swept Royce's legs out from under him.

Royce fell on his back in the mud, winded, and blinked as he looked up at Voyt, who stood over him, shaking his head.

"You focus too much on your foe's weapons," Voyt chided. "There are many weapons to a combatant. Swords, yes. But hands and feet, too."

Royce scrambled back to his feet and faced off again, breathing hard, wiping sweat from his eyes. Again Voyt charged, and again Royce blocked.

As Voyt drove him around the clearing, this time Royce tried to pay attention to what he'd been taught. He focused on his feet, and he began to feel himself moving more quickly, a bit more agile. He realized that Voyt was right. He managed to sidestep two blows that would have reached him before.

"Better," Voyt commented as he slashed down, just missing his arm. "But still too slow."

"This field is mud," Royce called back, slipping. "That's what's stopping me."

Voyt laughed.

"And do you think I am fighting on water?" he rebuked. "We share the same ground."

He snarled as he charged Royce with a fierce combination of slashes, seeming to rain down on him from all directions at once. It was all Royce could do to block them.

"Why do you think I brought you are here?" Voyt barked. "Do you think your opponent shall fight on a different ground than you? Do you think he, and he alone, holds the advantage? Do you think the Pits are made of grass and gravel? You'll be fighting in mud. And you'll likely die in mud. And from the looks of you, complaining the whole time."

Voyt let out a cry as he lunged again; this time Royce sidestepped and just missed the blow as Voyt went rushing past.

Royce was surprised at his own dexterity.

Voyt turned and faced him.

"Quick," he commented. "But another failure. You missed an opportunity. When you're close, you must forget your weapon and use your hands. You should have grabbed and thrown me as I passed by."

As he said these words he spun around and in one quick motion elbowed Royce in the back.

Royce stumbled forward, the pain blinding between his shoulder blades, and landed face first in the mud, winded. It felt as if a sledgehammer had smashed his back; he could scarcely believe one man could be that strong.

A moment later he felt strong hands lift him to his feet.

Royce stood there, face covered in mud, embarrassed, dejected.

"You will meet me here tomorrow before dawn," Voyt said. "Before the others wake. We shall try again."

Royce looked at him, shocked at the honor. He was filled with gratitude even while he was filled with pain.

"Why me?" he asked again.

Royce stared at Voyt and he found himself looking into the dark eyes the eyes of a killer. Yet they were also the eyes of a brave and true warrior, one Royce admired more than he could say.

"Because I see myself in you," Voyt said, "and I see what you could become."

Royce wondered how that could be possible. Voyt was the greatest warrior he had ever met. And a leader amongst men.

"If any one of this crop has a chance of surviving, it is you. The rest are already dead in my eyes."

Royce was floored by the compliment; he had no idea how he had even caught the attention of Voyt, who he had always thought looked down upon him. Yet at the same time Royce thought of Mark, and his heart dropped for his friend, as he imagined him not surviving.

Royce stared back.

"You really think I can survive?" he asked.

Voyt stared back, deadly serious.

"Probably not," he replied. "Not for long. But if I can prolong your life a little more, that will be enough."

Royce was baffled by this mysterious man.

"But why?" he asked. "Why do this for me?"

Voyt glanced down, and Royce realized he was looking at the burn mark on his forearm. He then looked back to Royce.

"For your father."

Royce stood there, completely baffled.

"My *father*?" Royce asked. "My father is but a peasant, a farmer in a small village. How would you, a great warrior, ever know my father?"

Slowly, seriously, Voyt shook his head.

"Your father is the only man who ever defeated me. And the only warrior I ever loved."

Voyt suddenly turned and marched off, leaving Royce standing there, filled with wonder.

Royce reached down and looked at his scar as if never seeing it before, and for the first time in his life, a new thought crossed his mind.

Who was his father?

And who, after all, was he?

CHAPTER TWENTY ONE

In the half light of the cell, Raymond stood back to back with his brothers, making his way over to one of the few windows there. It was just one of the lessons that life in the dungeon had taught them: never ask about someone else's life, never trust anyone who wasn't family, never give today what you might need to keep you alive tomorrow.

The dungeon had changed his brothers. Where before, they had both been healthy and well fed, now both of them looked gaunt with the lack of food. Lofen's broad frame had wasted away to half what it had been, while there hardly seemed to be anything of Garet left. Certainly not his smile. As for Raymond, he had a cough that came and wouldn't go easily, and pains in almost every part of his body from the fights that were the only way to survive down here.

"They're leaving us here until we die from it," Lofen said, not for the first time.

Raymond shrugged, the way he always shrugged when his brother said it. "Then we'll have to live and defy them, won't we?"

Lofen looked as though he might say something to that, but didn't, in the end. The three of them just made their way over to the small window to the dungeon, set high enough that Raymond had to stand on the others' shoulders to be able to see out.

Outside, castle life passed in its usual monotony. Servants came and went, carrying everything from candles to whole sides of beef that were enough to make Raymond's mouth water. Carts came and went, while in the background, always visible, was the cart with the post on it, there to take prisoners away to the gallows.

"They're setting up there," Raymond said.

"You think it will be us today?" Lofen asked.

How could Raymond answer that?

"No, not today," he said, trying to sound as confident as he could. "Come on, let me down, and you can each have a turn at looking."

They lowered Raymond back to the cell floor.

"And what about my turn?" a man demanded. He was big, and new, still brash enough to think that it mattered how strong he was in the outside world. "I've seen you boys, acting as if you own this place. Well, I'm here now."

He stepped forward, fists raised, and Raymond moved to meet him. When the man punched at him, Raymond swayed aside, punching back hard enough to snap the man's head back. Raymond caught him with an elbow as he closed in, driving the wind out of him. Lofen made as if he might join in, but Raymond waved him back. If the others thought that they could only fight when there were all three of them, they would try to strike at them one by one.

The man charged then, head down, like a bull. Raymond turned out of the way, shoving the man as hard as he could. He heard a crunch as his foe hit the wall head first, sliding down it into unconsciousness.

Around him, he could see the eyes of the other prisoners, men and women thrown into a large cell together to be largely forgotten, and after a while you prayed that they forgot you, because the ones they remembered either ended up screaming under torture, or dying in whatever way they'd devised today.

Raymond didn't know the names of the other prisoners. He didn't know what they were in there for, either. Asking questions wasn't safe in a place like this. Even on the occasions when there were screams deeper in the darkness, he and his brothers had learned not to get involved. They weren't like Royce, who would charge into danger blindly.

"It's my turn," Garet said.

"No," Lofen insisted. "It's mine."

"It's—"

A hammering on the iron door to the place cut off the argument before it could begin. It was a bizarre kind of parody of politeness, guards knocking on the door before entering not out of any kind of courtesy, but to terrify the prisoners into backing away.

"Back against the wall!" a guard yelled as the door creaked open. "All of you out of the way, or you'll regret it."

The torch he held was bright enough that it hurt Raymond's eyes after so long in the dark, leaving afterimages of flame whenever he looked away. Even like that though, it occurred to him that if all the prisoners in there were to act at once, they would easily be enough to overpower their guards.

None of them moved though. All they could hope for was for the guards' attention to pass over them. Raymond stood with his brothers, knowing that if today was the day when they were to die, there would be little that any of them could do about it.

Half a dozen guards moved through the cell, weapons drawn, looking around from one prisoner to the next, obviously stretching the moment out as much as they could. Raymond hated them for that, but then, he already had plenty else to hate them for.

"You!" a guard shouted, pointing, and Raymond hated himself for the relief he felt when that finger wasn't pointing at him.

The guards surged forward, grabbing a young woman from the mass of prisoners. She screamed, begging for mercy, but no one moved forward to help her. No one even began to. Raymond cursed himself for a coward, and started to take a step away from the wall, but one of the guards spun to him, raising a blade.

"Not your day today, boy, unless you want to make it that way," he snapped.

Raymond stood there, unwilling to back down. Garet stepped up beside him.

"Take us," his brother suggested. "If you want to hurt someone, take us."

Raymond stood ready to fight. He wasn't sure if they could do this, but he could try.

One of the guards kicked him back as he took a step back, and there were more there then, blades ready.

"Try again, and we'll gut you, then take her anyway, and slaughter the rest," the lead guard said.

Raymond felt Lofen's hand on his shoulder. Raymond stepped back. There was nothing he could do. They dragged the woman out, and she barely even fought. The dungeons had a way of breaking the people in them to the point where even death seemed preferable.

Raymond refused to let them do that to him, even though, as the guards dragged the prisoner out, he knew that sooner or later, that would be him and his brothers.

CHAPTER TWENTY TWO

Royce stood over Mark and held the tip of his wooden sword to his friend's throat as he lay on the ground before him, and smiled broadly. Mark, clearly disappointed, shook his head.

"Unfair," Mark said. "Can't I win just once?"

Royce lowered his sword and held out a hand; Mark took it, and Royce yanked him up.

"You fought very well, my friend," Royce said. "I just got lucky."

Mark frowned.

"And all the other times?" he asked. "Luck?"

"He has the edge because he cheats. Haven't you seen?"

It was a voice filled with meanness, and Royce turned to see Rubin step out from the circle of boys. The twins stepped forward behind him, and all three of them jumped down several feet into the muddy pit Royce had been sparring in—a replica of the Pits to come—and raised their wooden swords and faced him.

"Let's see how you can fight when it's three on one," Rubin added.

"I shall have your back," Mark said, raising his sword.

"No," Royce replied, stepping up alone. "It is my fight."

No sooner had Mark ascended the pit, than Rubin raised his sword and charged with a shout, the twins behind him, all clearly intent on killing Royce. The tension between them had been long simmering these past moons, and finally, it had exploded.

Royce was ready for it. After all these moons of training with Voyt he felt stronger than ever, ready to take on ten boys if needed, and he had been prepared for an ambush since the day he had arrived on this isle.

Royce raised his wooden sword and blocked the first blow, the clack of wood ringing out, then spun his sword around with lightning speed and jabbed Rubin in the stomach. Rubin keeled over with a whoomph.

Seth reached him at the same time, slashing for Royce's back, and Royce spun and blocked, then spun his sword around and struck upward, knocking his sword from his hand. He elbowed him in the face, dropping him.

Sylvan charged Royce, shouting, coming at him point out as if to run his sword through him. Royce sidestepped, slashed him across the stomach, then brought his sword around and brought it down on his back, sending him face-first in the mud.

Royce turned to Rubin, sword point out.

Rubin raised his hands.

"I give," he said, still on one knee.

Royce lowered his sword—yet the moment he did, Rubin suddenly threw a clump of mud into his eyes.

Royce, blinded, clawed at the mud, unable to see. The next moment he felt a boot in his chest and went stumbling back, landing on his back on the ground, disarmed.

"FIGHT!" cried the boys up above, watching.

A moment later Royce, still blinded and clawing at mud, felt Rubin's heavy weight atop him, his knees pinning down his shoulders. He then gasped, unable to breathe, as Rubin's fat palms wrapped around his throat.

Royce gripped the boy's wrists, struggling to breathe, but the boy had him pinned down.

"I've always hated you," Rubin seethed. He grinned. "And now the time has finally come to send you back to the farm from which you came. No one will notice you're gone."

Royce heard a sound and saw Mark jumping down into the pit. He rushed forward to save him—but the twins blocked his way and he fought furiously with them, trying to break through.

Royce, desperate, losing oxygen, knowing he was going to die, felt that feeling again. It rushed through him, from deep inside. It was a strength. A strength he did not understand. He did not need to understand it, he realized; he just needed to give in to it.

With a sudden surge of power, Royce managed to break his arms free of Rubin's grip, turn, and throw him off. He then rolled and pinned him down himself.

Royce choked Rubin as he himself had been choked. Rubin raised his arms and choked Royce, too. The two of them lay in the mud, the hatred coursing through them both, choking each other to death. Royce was losing air, but he took satisfaction in seeing Rubin losing more.

Suddenly, Royce felt a boot in his stomach. He felt himself kicked and the next thing he knew he went rolling in the mud.

He looked up to see several soldiers standing between him and Rubin, some stepping on Rubin's chest, too.

Voyt stepped up and shook his head, looking down at Royce as he spoke.

"As much as I'd love to see you two kill each other, today is not the day. We have more important business."

Hardly had he finished speaking the words than a horn sounded. It was the horn of gathering. Something important was happening.

Royce and the others got to their feet and gathered around Voyt. Rubin and the twins lined up on the far side of the circle, and Royce could see them fuming, vowing to get vengeance when the time came.

"BOYS!" Voyt boomed, and they all fell silent as he demanded their attention. "On this day some of you will become men. You will survive the final test, and your training will be over. Others of you will die. Your initiation has come."

He paced up and down the ranks, and Royce's heart pounded as he did, wondering what lay in store.

"You will journey from here as a group, descend into the Cave of Madness, and retrieve the Crystal Sword. It is guarded by a Mantra, a beast that has killed many before you, and will kill many more to come. For you, those few who have survived these moons, this is your reward. This is your privilege. A chance for a life fighting in the Pits. And a chance for a glorious death."

Royce caught Mark's look, his face filled with dread, as were the faces of the other boys.

"Beyond the Fields of Ore lies the entrance to the cave. You will go as one, and you will learn, finally, to fight as one. For if you do not, you will surely die. You will need each other, more than you ever have. If you fight together, you may survive. Only the worthy will return. And it is only the worthy whom I wish to see again."

A group of soldiers stepped forward, and Royce noticed that they each held a weapon, draped in a cloth of scarlet velvet. Voyt nodded and they removed the cloths, and Royce gasped to see twelve stunning swords revealed, shining, with platinum hilts, crafted of a finer metal than he'd ever seen.

Each soldier stepped forward and handed each boy one sword. Royce reached out and took his, holding the hilt with one hand, its blade with the other. He was in awe. It was a thing of majesty. Its steel was black, carved with the insignia of the Red Isle, while its hilt was flanked by long, silver prongs. Its blade was long and sharp, the sharpest he'd ever seen, made of a metal he did not know. Royce raised the sword, and it felt like lightning in his hands. It was the greatest weapon he had ever held.

"These are the weapons of men," Voyt said. "Not of boys. For it is men you have become here on the Red Isle."

He paced, looking them up and down.

"Here, on the Red Isle," Voyt continued, "we give our initiates swords *before* they are initiated. That way if you die, you will die holding your reward in your hand."

He paced up and down the ranks, and Royce examined the sword, gleaming in the morning light, and felt himself welling with pride. Whatever happened, whatever was to come, he had earned this, and no one could take that away from him.

"In the Cave of Madness," Voyt boomed, "you shall find the scabbards and swords of many boys who held swords like these before you, and who died before you. They are men, too. There is no shame in dying. Only shame in fear."

A horn sounded again, and as the group dissembled, Royce found himself exchanging glances with the eleven other boys, who all looked stunned. They all looked as if they were staring death in the face.

A Mantra, Royce thought. He had read about them as a boy. A horrible and cruel monster. A beast of legend. He shook his head. There was no way they could survive.

Slowly the group of boys came together, and as one, they turned away from the clearing and began the long trek across the plains. One foot in front of the other, they marched across the barren wasteland before them, under the cold, brilliant sunlight of another dawn. All walked in silence.

They walked slowly, reluctantly, across the wasteland, even Rubin and the twins, for the first time not harassing anyone. It was a solemn death march across the barren rocks, each step taking them closer to the cave, somewhere at the far end of the isle.

It was when the sun hung high in the sky that Royce looked up and stopped short with the others. They stood at the edge of a precipice. As he looked down, a gale of wind struck him in the face. Royce stood there, gaping with the others. None said a word.

There below sat a massive mountain, and in its side, a gaping entrance, a hundred yards wide and high, to a cave. It appeared to be the entrance to hell itself.

There arose an awful smell from the cave, blown on the wind all the way to here. Royce could feel the waves of heat, too, coming from what must have been its breath. He felt the tremor beneath his feet, heard the snorts of a massive creature lurking far below, somewhere in the blackness.

He looked over at his brothers-in-arms, and from their faces it looked as if some of them had already died.

113

Without another word, they all took the first step and descended together, as one, into the very depths of hell.

CHAPTER TWENTY THREE

Genevieve stood in the bleachers, high up, towering over the crowd below, and looked away in revulsion as the crowd roared at the spectacle. The stadium shook as men and women jumped to their feet, cheering. She couldn't believe the viciousness that so moved these people. What she would give to be anywhere but here.

Genevieve turned to go when she suddenly felt a hand grab her arm roughly and yank her back.

She looked over to see Moira, her sister-in-law, looking back sternly, unnoticed amidst the chaos.

Moira quietly shook her head.

"You are a noble now," she warned. "Act the part. Unless you want to find yourself locked in a dungeon."

Genevieve stood there, numb, and slowly turned and looked back down at the spectacle. There, below her, was the muddy fighting pit, its steep walls rising twenty feet so its fighters could not escape. In its center, on the muddy earth, lay a man, dead, face up, a spear in his chest. Next to him stood another man, wearing a grotesque mask shaped like a lion. He looked up, raising his arms and beating his chest, soaking in the adulation of the crowd. He paraded around the pit like a peacock, having just murdered this man in cold blood.

The crowd could not get enough, and each cheer was like a knife through Genevieve's heart. She hated this place. Hated these nobles. Hated everything this savage kingdom was about.

What she hated most of all were her thoughts of Royce. There, below, was his future, awaiting him. It was awful. Worse than death. And it was all because of her.

Perhaps that was why Altfor had dragged her here, Genevieve thought. She looked over and saw him standing there, clapping, his face so smugly self-satisfied like all the others. She could hardly believe she was married to this man. *Married.* The thought turned her stomach. Six moons had slowly passed, too slowly, an agony of waiting to hear from Royce. Yet no word ever came. She did not know if he was even alive. Yet she dreamed of him every night. In most dreams he was reaching for her, his fingertips grazing hers, just out of her grasp.

Genevieve sighed, shaking the thought from her mind. It could be worse, she told herself. At least Altfor had not made her sleep with him. He'd even allowed her a separate chamber, a separate bed, and this allowed her to feel like the prisoner she wanted to be. She wanted to share the isolation and pain that Royce felt.

Genevieve looked over and noticed a girl standing on the other side of Altfor. She was young, and stunningly beautiful. Genevieve had seen her many times before, always getting close to Altfor. She saw her drape a gentle arm around his, and she noticed that her husband did not shake it off. The girl looked at him with love and affection as she batted her eyes up at him.

"You're a fool," came a voice.

Genevieve turned to see Moira staring at the girl with her.

"He will find someone else, you know," Moira continued. "He's a man, and men have needs. They do not like to be scorned. Keep ignoring him, and you will be discarded."

Genevieve smiled.

"Good," she replied. "There's nothing I wish for more."

Moira frowned and shook her head.

"You still don't understand," she replied. "Nobles are obsessed with titles. You're a *wife* now. You're part of this family forever. Whether you realize it or not."

Genevieve struggled to understand.

"But you just said if he tired of me, he would let me go."

Moira shook her head.

"He would take another woman, true, yet you would never truly be free," she replied. "They could never allow you to be out there, free, marrying someone else. Especially not Royce. Not after all this. It would shame them. They would hide you away somewhere. In a dungeon, most likely. Never to be heard of again."

"Good," Genevieve insisted. "I do not wish to be free if my love is not."

Moira shook her head again.

"You are a bigger fool than I thought," she replied. "You are Royce's only hope. If you are locked in a dungeon, what hope will he ever have?"

Genevieve blinked, pondering her sister-in-law's words.

"But how does my being married, being a noble, help him? It has done nothing for him thus far."

Moira frowned.

"Because you know nothing of the ways of nobles. And you have not even bothered to learn. Nobles have power. Unlimited power, more than you could ever imagine. If you were a true noble wife and mother, beloved by the family, you could do anything you wish. With the snap of your fingers you could command anyone you wish. Save anyone you wish."

Genevieve felt her heart beat faster for the first time since arriving here. She leaned in closer to Moira.

"Yes," Moira said, excited. "You'd have power over Royce's life. Do you wish to save your beloved? Or would you rather wallow away in a dungeon somewhere in a cloud of self-pity, while Royce, too, suffers and dies?"

Genevieve pondered her words and felt a surge of optimism. For the first time, she wanted to live again.

"Of course I want to save Royce," she replied. "I would give my life for him."

Moira nodded.

"And do you really think you will be able to save him, to gain any power at all, if you allow your husband to go into another woman's arms?"

Genevieve thought about that.

"Don't you see?" Moira pressed. "Before you lies the steppingstone to power. If you want it all, you must stop running from your role. You must embrace it."

Moira retreated back into the roaring crowd, and as they all began to disperse, the fights over, Genevieve turned and looked at Altfor. There he stood, the girl still with an arm on him. As she looked, she suddenly had a whole new perspective. Moira's words rang in her mind and she realized that she was right. This was an opportunity before her. A lost opportunity.

She must go to Altfor at once. Embrace him, love him.

Even if it was the thing she wished for least in the world.

Through love comes power.

CHAPTER TWENTY FOUR

Royce marched with the group of boys into the Cave of Madness, taking one step at a time down the steep, gravelly slope until the absolute blackness nearly consumed them. The weak sunlight from high above filtered down, its rays getting weaker with each step, hardly giving them any light to see by. Mark marched beside him, the two of them in the middle of the group, the rest of the boys in front and behind them, all of them marching as one, down into the monster's lair.

Finally, they were all one unit. They marched as a group, staying close, swords held out before them with shaking hands, the fear in the air palpable. The tunnel was cavernous, a hundred yards wide, the sound of their boots echoing, merging with the sound of something dripping from the ceiling. Something scurried in the darkness before them, then quickly disappeared. Royce did not like to think what it may have been.

Worst of all was the smell. It smelled like rot down here, Royce turning his head away as the tremendous heat came up in waves, carrying the noxious smell. He was afraid to consider its source: the noxious breath of the monster, waiting for them. It only deepened his sense of dread.

A distant rumble, like thunder, rolled off the walls from somewhere far away, seeming to fill the entire place, and Royce turned to Mark, who looked back. He felt his own palms begin to sweat. Whatever that was, there was no way they could defeat it.

Royce saw Rubin up ahead, flanked by the twins, for the first time not staring back at Royce with hatred. Instead, he stared straight ahead, frozen in fear. He was too busy marching to his death to worry about bullying others.

For the first time, the twelve of them were all in this together. They had survived the ship ride here together, had survived the march of the worthy, had survived these past twelve moons here, and had all bonded—except, of course, for Rubin and the twins, who had always remained aloof. But Royce and the eight others had formed a bond deeper than friendship; they were now like brothers. They were all marching to their deaths as a family. Royce would die for any of these boys, and he knew that they would die for him. Somehow, that made it all the more bearable.

It was something that Rubin and the twins had never understood, something that they would miss out on.

"If we are to survive this, we must remain close together."

Royce did not need to turn to know who was speaking; he recognized the voice. It was Altos, walking up beside him, a tall muscular, clean-shaven boy with short black hair and black eyes. All the boys looked up to and respected Altos, Royce amongst them. Altos had always presented himself as a leader, had always taken the high road, had always been the first to volunteer. He, Royce, and Mark had become fast friends from the start.

"We must face the beast as one," Altos continued.

"If the beast should attack," chimed in Sanos, a fearless, wiry boy with flaming red hair, endlessly loyal to Royce and the others, "we must work as a team, some of us distracting while others attack."

"You have your strategies, we have ours," interjected Rubin, turning back, glaring. "We do not need you. I can fight alone. If you're too scared to do so, you can do as you please."

"You can fight alone and you can die alone," Altos hissed back. "I care nothing for you."

The tension increased between the nine boys and Rubin and the twins, and Royce's apprehension deepened at the fractured group. He knew Altos was right: only if they worked together would they survive this. And they were not together as of now; they were a group of nine and a group of three.

"Go your way and we will go ours," interjected the twins. "We'll see who survives."

Rubin and the twins split off from the group, forking off to the right, deeper into the cave, creating distance from themselves and the group.

"The beast, after all, will look for the larger group—and that means you," Rubin added, laughing as they disappeared into the blackness, now just a voice.

Royce shook his head as they marched ahead, veering off in different directions.

"We're better off," Mark said, voicing all of their thoughts. "Now at least we are truly one unit."

Royce's heart beat faster as they descended deeper and deeper into the cave, lower and lower, the light becoming more diffused, harder to see by. There soon came a crunching sound beneath his feet, and Royce looked down and squinted in the darkness. He realized with a start he was stepping on bones. The bones, he assumed, of boys who had come before him.

"Look!" Sanos called out in horror.

Royce looked over and watched Sanos bend over and pick up a sword, extracting it from the grip of a skeletal hand. Royce gulped. It was the same sword he was holding. The sword of a boy who had come before him, who had been sent on a mission just like this.

Royce scanned the cave floor and saw there was not just one sword—but dozens. This place was not a battleground; it was a burial ground.

This was where trainees were sent to die.

Royce suddenly wondered if any of the boys had ever returned.

The group continued on, silent, the air filled with nothing but the sound of boots crunching on bones, and the rumbling of the beast, somewhere in the distance, growing louder by the moment. The heat and noxious air was becoming stifling. Royce soon found himself sweating, whether from heat or fear he did not know.

"If I don't survive and you do, and you ever return to the mainland," Mark said, his voice filled with fear, "return to my village of Ondor and tell my sister that I love her."

Royce turned to see Mark looking straight ahead in the darkness, eyes wide with fear.

"And tell her that I am sorry I let her down."

Royce shook his head.

"You can tell her yourself, my friend," Royce replied. "You are not dying on this day. And neither am I."

Yet as Royce continued walking, he wondered if his words rang true.

Suddenly an awful roar erupted, one that raised the hair on Royce's neck. He stopped in his tracks with the others, and as he looked up, what emerged from the depths of the blackness only increased his sense of dread.

It was unlike anything he had ever seen. The beast resembled a bear, with its long, brown fur, yet was ten times the size, with a single, glowing red eye, sharpened yellow claws, and two long horns protruding from the sides of its head. It stood on its hind legs, towering over them, snarled, and roared again, the sound nearly shattering Royce's ears.

Royce could barely hear himself think, the sound echoing all around them. The roar was followed by the sound of squeaking, and Royce looked up to see thousands of little creatures, resembling bats, flying away in a flock, clearly trying to get away from the monster.

In the distance, on the far side of the beast, Royce felt his heart pound as he spotted the Crystal Sword, the very weapon his masters demanded they retrieve. Looking at it now, Royce realized how impossible it was. There was no way they could get past this monster—much less survive here.

Royce heard a crunching noise and was shocked as he turned to see Leithna suddenly turn and run in panic. Royce was disgusted at his cowardice, yet if there was anyone he would expect to run it would be him; he had barely survived his training. Royce could understand. That beast was hideous enough to inspire fear in even the most intrepid heart.

Royce watched in horror as the beast suddenly lunged forward, shockingly fast given its size, and set its sights on Leithna as he fled across the cave. Within a few bounds he had reached him, and as it swiped with its long arms, its yellow claws slashed his back in half.

Leithna shrieked and collapsed face-first to the ground in a pool of blood. Without pausing, the beast picked him up in its claws and put him in his mouth, swallowing him whole.

"Attack!" Altos called out.

Altos ran forward fearlessly, raising his sword, and Royce joined the others as they all charged as one, raising their swords in a great outcry. As they closed in, Royce, his heart pounding, continued running until he reached the beast and stabbed it in its thigh. Mark and the others boys reached it, too, slashing and stabbing it across its legs and shins, as high as they could reach. Altos hurled his sword, sending it spinning end over end through the air until it lodged deep into the beast's thigh.

The beast leaned back and shrieked in pain. Given all the expert wounds, Royce expected it to stumble back and fall; after all, they had timed it perfectly and had attacked with all they'd had. Royce was proud of his brothers. They were truly one unit now.

Yet, to Royce's shock, the beast merely reached down, grabbed Altos in one hand, raised him up, and moved to put him into his mouth, as if to swallow him whole. As the beast squeezed its hand into a fist, Royce heard a sickening cracking sound, and he realized it was Altos's ribs cracking. Altos shrieked in agony.

Royce acted quickly, knowing he had but moments if he wished to save his friend. He planted his feet, reached back with his sword, took aim, and hurled it.

He watched it sail end over end through the air and finally find a place in the beast's eye.

The beast shrieked and then dropped Altos. He fell twenty feet through the air and landed on the hard cave floor, groaning, perhaps cracking more ribs. But at least he was alive.

The beast, roaring in fury, pulled the sword from his eye and, blinded, stomped around madly, trying to kill anything in its path.

Royce's brothers ran, trying to escape the massive feet that came down like hammers, creating craters in the earth. Royce watched in horror as five of them could not escape quickly enough and were crushed and killed. Royce's heart ached as he saw his new friend Sanos lying there, amongst the unlucky ones, crushed into the earth.

That left six dead, and Altos wounded. Which left Royce and Mark the only ones standing. Royce could scarcely believe it. All these brave boys, boys he had trained with and lived with all of these moons, all of them killed so quickly.

The beast turned toward them, as if sensing them in the blackness.

Royce detected motion and he looked out of the corner of his eye to see Rubin and the twins creep forward in the shadows. Now that the beast was blinded, they raised their swords and rushed forward and jabbed them all the way through the beast's thick feet, pinning it to the ground.

The beast roared, infuriated as it was stuck.

Royce expected the beast to stay pinned, yet to his surprise it managed to lift one foot out of the ground, then another. It bunched its hands into fists, raised them high above its face, and brought one down blindly. Seth looked up in horror as its fist came down and smashed him into the earth.

The beast then roared, reached out, and somehow managed to sense Sylvan, snatching him up in the air and in one quick motion eating him alive, drowning out his awful shrieks as the boy entered his mouth.

The only who remained now were Royce, Mark, Altos—lying on the ground, immobile—and Rubin. Rubin, clearly sensing an opportunity, ran for the Crystal Sword at the far end of the cave. Royce realized with indignation that Rubin meant to snatch the sword and run out of the cave himself, while all the others died down here.

Rubin reached the sword and grabbed it and prepared to run—when the beast detected him. It spun, swiped its huge claws, and snatched Rubin up. It held him high, bringing him close as if to eat him.

Royce knew that Rubin deserved to die; even so, he did not feel he could allow it to happen. Even though Rubin had behaved terribly, had been an awful person, Rubin was still his brother-in-arms, after all. And it was not Royce's way to sit there and let a fellow boy die, even if he deserved it.

Royce let out a great cry, feeling a rush of determination, and without thinking of his own safety, he rushed forward, grabbed a sword off the ground, and leapt into the air. As he jumped he felt a great heat rise within his body, felt the power come to him. He found himself leaping higher and higher in the air, twenty, thirty feet. It was surreal. It was almost as if he were flying.

Royce raised the sword as he flew and, palms throbbing with power, he brought it down right for the beast's chest, plunging it in.

The beast shrieked. It stared down as if in shock and dropped Rubin, who landed on the ground far below. It then reached down and grabbed Royce.

But Royce held onto the sword with all his might, dangling in the air, impaling it in its chest, refusing to let go even as he felt the beast's claws wrap around him. Slowly, the beast's claws tightened around him, squeezing the life out of him. Royce did not know how much more pressure he could stand before he broke into pieces. He knew he was about to die.

In one decisive motion, Royce reached back and broke the beast's grip, knocking its arms off him, finally able to breathe again. He then let out a great battle cry, pulled out the sword, swung it around, and chopped off the beast's head.

The beast fell backward, like a great tree falling, and Royce held on as it landed flat on the ground, Royce crashing on top of him.

Finally, it was dead.

Royce stood on the beast's chest, holding his sword, breathing hard, his palms still vibrating. Slowly, he turned and looked around.

In the dim light of the cave he saw Mark, Altos, and Rubin, the only three other survivors, staring back at him, eyes filled with wonder. With more than wonder. With awe. They all looked to Royce as if he were a god.

Royce stood there, arms trembling, barely able to believe what he'd just done.

And wondering, even more, who he was.

CHAPTER TWENTY FIVE

Royce stood before the raging bonfire, the blaze crackling even above the sound of the ocean winds whipping off the coast of the Red Isle, and as he stared into the flames, he realized how surreal it was to be alive. Mark stood on one side of him, Altos, nursing his broken ribs, on the other, and Rubin beside them, the four of them the only survivors of the boys in that batch, standing there amidst the broad circle of soldiers while others, who had clearly completed their training previously, looked on. It was a victorious night, but a solemn one, and Royce could feel the spirits of his dead brothers all around him.

Royce looked up and examined the hardened faces of the men around him, the toughest men he had ever seen, men as hard as this place, men he respected more than any in the world. It was hard to believe these were the same men who had greeted him when he had first arrived on this isle twelve moons ago. Had they changed that much? Or had he?

Royce examined the blade of the Crystal Sword, which he held in his hands, examining it in wonder. How many boys had had to die for this sword? he wondered. How many years had that beast guarded it?

He could see the men, Voyt in their center, staring back at him, and could see that they were all, finally, impressed. They looked at him now with a new sense of respect. They looked at them not as boys, but as men. As warriors. As fighters ready to leave this place, to be sent to the pits.

That thought made Royce pause as Voyt stepped forward. He held a bunch of straws in his hand, held out as if they were a weapon.

"Your training has concluded," he said, "and now you are worthy to learn your place in things. The Red Isle is seen as a place that trains men so that they may die with greater honor in the Pits. So that their criminals may die. Yet some of you, a very few, one in a dozen groups, may have a chance to be more. There can be no pattern to this, and there is no space for all of you, so luck is all that is left to you. When I come to you, choose a straw, and hope that it is a long one."

He started to go around the ranks of the boys who had gone through the training, both in their contingent and others. Royce saw boy after boy picking short straws, groans and winces coming from them as they did. He saw Rubin pick a short straw and cast it on the ground in disgust.

It was his turn then. He felt... somehow, he felt as if this moment meant something, as if it had always been meant. Royce thought of the mark on his arm; the one Voyt had recognized. Perhaps this was the moment when it turned out to mean something more. He reached out blindly, letting instinct guide him as he drew from the bundle Voyt held.

He heard the trainer sigh in disappointment as he drew a short straw.

"I had thought... I had hoped..."

"Hoped what?" Royce asked, guessing that this might be the last chance he had.

Voyt grabbed him hard, the way he might as if threatening someone, yet when he spoke, his words were soft, not filled with venom.

"The Red Isle is a place of training, and not just for the Pits. We use it as an excuse to find men to join a guard worthy of a king." He shook his head sadly. "But your straw was short. Your destiny lies elsewhere."

Voyt stepped back and went back to handing out straws. No one picked a long one this time, and Royce could feel the disappointment hanging over their group like a cloud. Their training had finally concluded, but what now?

Voyt stood facing them.

"And now you shall leave us," Voyt said, his voice dark, somber. "You shall face the Pits. You shall become entertainment for the kingdom."

He sighed, and Royce detected sorrow in that sigh.

"And yet," he continued, "you will never be entertainment to *us*. You are a part of our brotherhood. Remember that always, as you fight. As fighters come to face you from all corners of the earth, remember what you have learned here. Remember this place, remember the brothers you have lost, and fight not only for yourselves, but for them. And as you die, know that you have earned this great honor. For having a chance to die in glory is indeed one of the greatest honors a man could hope for."

Voyt stepped aside, and as he did, Royce spotted a light in the distance in the black of night. It was dim, far off, bobbing, and it took him a few moments to realize what it was: a lantern, swinging

125

on a ship. A small wooden ship sat anchored in the rough waters near the shoreline, and Royce, stunned, looked over at Voyt, who nodded back with a knowing look.

"The time has come to leave," he affirmed.

Royce could not help but feel a mixture of triumph and sadness; of longing to be back home, and despair for the death to come. As much as he had hated this isle, he had also become a warrior here, had learned more about himself than he'd ever cared to know. A part of him was loath to leave. Voyt, as harsh as he was, had become something of a father figure to him. He was as close to being a father as Royce had ever had. Royce realized he would miss him.

"Law requires us to shackle you," Voyt continued. "I shall not. You may not be free in the eyes of the kingdom, but you are free in ours. For all true warriors are free. Sail back, fight, die a glorious death, and make us all proud."

The men parted ways, and one at a time, Royce and the others, wearing their new breastplates, wielding their new swords, began to walk toward the coastline, toward the ship waiting in the blackness. Royce fell in last, and as he went, he heard rocks crunching and looked over; he was surprised to find Voyt walking beside him.

"I shall accompany you," Voyt said. Royce thought he could detect sadness in his voice.

They walked for a long time in silence on the craggy isle, Royce wondering what his mentor had to say, if anything. Perhaps they would just walk the entire way in silence.

"Soon the waves will bring another crop of boys," Voyt said, his voice pensive. "And soon those boys will meet their deaths."

Royce looked over and saw Voyt was looking straight ahead as they walked, as if examining the black ocean for something he could not find.

"You are apart from the others," he added.

Royce pondered his words, wondering what they meant. He recalled his mysterious power, recalled how he had always felt as if the others were looking at him askance. How, after all, had he defeated that beast? How had he done so many things he should not have been able to do?

Royce looked down and studied his necklace, shining in the moonlight, and it occurred to him to ask Voyt a question he had feared to ask his entire stay here.

"My father," Royce said, nervous, his voice tremulous. "You never told me about him."

There came a long silence, one so long that Royce was sure Voyt would never respond, as they continued to walk for the coast.

But then, finally, Voyt sighed.

"The time is not right," he said. "You are not ready. I can tell you only that you have a great legacy behind you. And a great destiny before you."

Voyt suddenly grabbed hold of Royce, gripping his arm tight as they reached the boat. As the others walked up the plank, he stood there and turned his intense eyes on Royce. Royce saw death in those eyes. A killer's eyes.

"When the time comes," he said with urgency, "you will know what to do. The realm depends on you. Do not let your father down."

Royce stared back, baffled, as Voyt turned and abruptly strode off, back toward the raging bonfire in the distance, back toward his men on the barren isle. What had he meant?

Royce turned and saw his three brothers-in-arms awaiting him, standing on the long plank leading to the ship. He joined them, and the four of them boarded the wildly rocking ship together.

The moment they did, the plank was raised, and a soldier stepped forward and chopped the rope. The ship set off into the night, the waters lifting it and carrying it away, and Royce stood at the stern, watching the Red isle disappear. It was hard to believe they were leaving this place. This island had given them much, but had taken more. They were all haunted men now.

The waters picked up speed, and Royce knew the mainland was somewhere out there, waiting for them. His heart raced with excitement.

Genevieve, he thought, looking out into the night. *I'm coming for you.*

CHAPTER TWENTY SIX

Genevieve stood outside Altfor's chamber, the fort quiet so late into the night, raised the heavy iron ring, and knocked. It sounded hollow, too loud on the thick oak, and it was odd to think of herself standing here, in a drafty stone corridor, and knocking on her husband's door to be let in.

She stood there, waiting in the silence, her heart pounding. So stupid of her, she realized, not to do this sooner. She only prayed it was not now too late. What if that girl was now behind that door, wrapped in her husband's arms? What if Altfor opened the door and slammed it in her face? What chance would she ever have of saving Royce then?

She stood there, waiting, hoping it was not too late.

Genevieve reached up to knock again, but this time, before she could grab the knocker, the door opened with a creak. There stood Altfor, eyes narrowed with suspicion, silk robe pulled tight. Genevieve watched his eyes widen in surprise when he saw her.

He paused ever so briefly in the door, and as he did, Genevieve's heart pounded.

Please don't let it be too late.

Then, slowly, he took a step back, and to her immense relief, he said:

"Come in."

Genevieve walked in as he closed the door behind. She reached back and bolted it, and he looked at her in surprise.

She then quickly scanned the room, praying for no signs of the girl. She was relieved to find none.

Genevieve took a deep breath. It was just her and Altfor. There they stood, in the dim light of the torches, nothing but the soft crackle of the fireplace as the moonlight shone through the window.

"A funny question for my wife," he said, his voice soft, "but why have you come here?"

She stared at him, took a step forward, and, hands trembling, heart pounding, reached up and gently placed her palms on his shoulders.

"To be with you," she replied, her voice tremulous.

His eyes widened in surprise. He stared for a long time, and she could feel him summing her up, as if gauging her to see if she were genuine.

Finally, he reached out and took her hand.

"Promise me one thing though," Genevieve said.

"You are my wife," Altfor said. "I have already made the promises that matter."

"Please, Altfor," Genevieve asked.

He seemed to relent for a moment.

"What promise do you want?" he asked.

"Promise me that you'll be kind to the peasants," she said. "I know what it's like to be one, to live in fear. You said before that you aren't your brother, so promise me."

He nodded. "You are a selfless woman, Genevieve, and I'll promise you what you want. Just tell me one thing. Tell me that you want me."

Genevieve steeled herself. She had to do this. She had to be the person who *could* do this.

She leaned forward to kiss him. "I want you more than anything."

Altfor tightened his grip on her hand, and led her to the bed.

Genevieve, heart pounding, allowed herself to be led, each step like a knife in her heart. She did not want this. But for Royce, she would do anything.

He guided her into bed, and as he began to undress her, she tried with all she had to hide her tears, to put her mind anywhere but here.

And as Altfor pulled the covers over them, she had only one final thought:

Royce. Forgive me.

CHAPTER TWENTY SEVEN

Royce stood at the bow holding the weathered rail, and as he studied the crashing waves, their spray hitting his new breastplate, he wondered what his future might bring. On one side of him stood Mark, on the other, Altos, the three of them standing there as one, looking out at the infinity of the ocean. They'd been through so much together, the three of them. Moons of grueling training, crossing the ocean here and back, losing so many friends and brothers-in-arms. They had formed a bond that was stronger than friends, stronger than brothers. They were family now. They were all each other had left in the world. And they were the only ones in the world who could understand what they had each gone through.

It was hard to believe that they had set out from Sevania so many moons ago, on a ship packed with hundreds of boys, so full they could barely move. And now here they were, the sole survivors, returning alone. In one sense, they had been the lucky ones. And yet still, death awaited them. So had they been lucky after all?

Royce studied the rolling waves, their ship rising higher and lower in the ocean, and tried not to contemplate what awaited him. He knew he would soon be thrown into the Pits. Dying did not frighten him, not anymore. What bothered him was that he would be forced to kill others, for sport. It didn't seem like a good enough reason; it protected no one; it served no cause or greater good. He hated, too, knowing his friends would die, sent to their own deaths, all their training there for nothing more than to ensure that they lasted a little longer before the end.

As he felt the spray of the ocean on his face, Royce's thoughts turned to what mattered even more than all of this: Genevieve. She, after all, was the reason he had been shipped off to this isle in the first place. For her, he would do it all over again. Was she waiting for him? What had become of her?

Images of her floated before his face, and his heart quickened at the chance to perhaps see her, to see his family, again. He did not want to raise his hopes. They'd be physically closer, on the same continent, and yet he would obviously not be escorted to her presence; she would probably not even know he had returned. Instead he would be dropped into a pit somewhere to fight and to die, and ironically, though closer to her, he would likely never see her again. The thought pained him to no end.

"Will you kill?"

Royce looked over, snapping out of his reverie, to see Altos standing beside him, also staring out to sea, his eyes also filled with uncertainty. It was a soft question, to the point.

Would he kill?

There was no question he would fight gloriously, would fight with honor and pride, would fight to defend himself in battle. Of course he would.

But that wasn't the question, Royce knew. It was: would he kill another human being for sport? Because their masters told them to? Would he give them that satisfaction?

Killing them would feed the machine, would fuel the masters' entertainment, would make him no better than any of the others. It would give the masters what they wanted: complete control over him once and for all.

To *not* kill, though, would mean his own death. It would also make him a coward in the eyes of all his fellow citizens.

"I do not wish to die a coward," Mark chimed in. "If someone comes to kill me, I don't see what choice I have."

A long silence followed.

"And yet, to kill them," Altos said, "is to give the kingdom what it wants."

"What choice do we have?" Mark countered.

Royce stood there, gripping the rail, looking out as the waves changed from blue to green and sharing the same thoughts as his brothers. They were being put in an impossible situation. A situation worse than death.

"If we kill someone just for sport," Altos said, after a long silence, "what happens to us is worse than death. Our soul is killed."

Royce could not help but think that Altos was right. He glanced back at the soldiers guarding the ship, and he wondered again if there was some way to escape. Dozens of them lined the rails, weapons at the ready. And dozens more, he knew, would be awaiting them on shore.

"And if you could escape?" Mark asked, catching his glance and reading his thoughts. "What would you do?"

"Free Genevieve," Royce answered without hesitation.

Mark nodded in approval.

"How would you free her?" Altos pressed.

"I would kill any soldiers in my way and get her out."

"So you *would* kill, then," Altos said with a grin.

Royce shook his head.

"Killing for justice is not killing for sport," he replied.

There came a long silence, their ship gently rising and falling, until finally Mark spoke.

"Perhaps they shall assign us together," Mark said. "Perhaps we shall be put in the same pit, and fight side by side."

Altos shook his head.

"They will make us fight separately. They don't want to risk us winning. They just want a good show out of us before we die."

The thought made Royce's heart fall.

"Let us make a pact, then," Altos said. "If one of us should break free, he will seek out the others, and the three of us shall try to break free together."

Altos put out his arm, Mark clasped it, and Royce clasped it, too. It was a pact between brothers. There was nothing, Royce knew, more sacred than that.

*

Many hours later, late into the night, Royce still stood there, at the rail, alone, long after the others had fallen asleep. He stood frozen, looking up at the moon, out at the waters, watching the waves rise and fall, numb to the world. He felt as if he were counting the minutes left to his life, and he kept thinking of Genevieve. He wondered if she were awake now, staring at the same moon. He wondered if he could use his skills to defeat his captors. No, it was too uncertain. The instincts he had for battle seemed to come and go, and here, on the ship, it might make too little difference.

Royce was looking out into the remains of the night when he heard a creaking behind him, and he turned, on guard, remembering Rubin. He was, after all, somewhere on the ship. Royce turned, drawing his sword, ready.

Rubin stood there, several feet away, walking slowly toward him, and he put his hands up innocently in the air.

"I'm not here to fight you," Rubin explained. He looked down to the ground, clearly shamed. "Only to thank you."

Royce examined him, and he noticed Rubin looked like a different man. He looked broken, humbled.

Royce slowly sheathed his sword. He studied Rubin as he looked back up.

"You saved my life," Rubin said in disbelief. "When you did not need to. When you had every reason *not* to. I can't stop thinking about it. I've come to ask why."

Royce looked at him, startled. He had never expected this.

"Because every life is worth saving," Royce said. "Even those of your enemy. Even those of the bullies who have tormented others."

Rubin stared back, clearly taken aback, then slowly nodded.

"I owe you my life," he said. "When you saved me, something changed within me. It made me realize…"

He trailed off. He stepped forward, next to Royce, and gripped the rail and looked out to sea. Knuckles white, he remained silent for a long while.

"It made me realize…how wrong I have been. What a fool I have been. How ashamed I am. I am a changed man. I know I cannot expect your forgiveness, but I want to ask you for it."

Royce was shocked by his words. He had not expected this. He studied Rubin for a long time, and finally concluded he was genuine.

"The way I acted, the way I treated everyone," Rubin said. "It was because I was…afraid. Afraid that others would treat *me* that way. It was defensive. I was raised by a father who would beat me every night. My mother left me when I was young. My brothers tormented me. Being tormented…it was all I'd ever known."

He sighed.

"It wasn't until you saved me that I realized that people can be otherwise in this world. *You* saved me. More than this entire isle, more than all those moons of training, your one act of grace is what saved me."

He took a deep breath and faced Royce.

"I know I don't deserve your forgiveness," he said, "but I need to ask you for it anyway."

Royce stared back, unsure what to say. Clearly, Rubin was a changed man.

Finally, Royce nodded.

"I harbor no ill feelings towards you," Royce said. "But it is not I alone from whom you need forgiveness. There are a great number of boys you tormented. Including Altos and Mark."

Rubin nodded in agreement.

"I shall ask forgiveness of them all. I have changed. You must believe me."

Royce looked at him more intently, and his words felt true.

"I believe you," Royce replied.

Rubin stepped close.

"I want you to know that you have a friend in me for life," Rubin added, holding out his arm.

Royce wondered briefly if this were a trick, until he saw the sincerity in his eyes. Rubin was indeed a changed man. A broken man. A man who had faced death and who had not expected to come out the other side.

Royce reached out and clasped his arm in return, and in that grip, he sensed he'd found, in the most unlikely of places, with the most unlikely of people, a friend for life.

CHAPTER TWENTY EIGHT

Genevieve walked slowly with Altfor, arm in arm, across the wide marble plaza at the top of the palace grounds, taking in the world of opulence. The marble stretched as far as the eye could see and was interlaced with formal gardens, bubbling fountains, flowering orchards—a true picture of luxury. Of everything her people had been denied. She looked down at herself, dressed in the finest silks, wearing precious jewelry, and was surprised to realize that she had become indistinguishable from the royals. It made her hate herself even more.

What had she become?

Ever since that fateful night when she had gone to Altfor's bed, had given herself to him, had stopped resisting and had accepted her role as his wife, things had changed radically for her. She had been showered with everything her heart could want and more, down to the heavy jewels she wore around her neck. She had been allowed to leave the castle grounds, to roam where she wished. She'd been afforded the highest respect not only by Altfor, but by the entire royal family, down to the castle guards. They all looked upon her, she could see, as one of their own.

Yet the more she was given, the more respect she was afforded, the sadder she became. She did not want any of it. She only wanted Royce.

It was a funny feeling. Her entire life she had been viewed as a peasant, like all the people she had grown up with. As she walked the grounds and they bowed to her, she felt uncomfortable; she could not help but feel as if they had her confused with someone else.

What felt even stranger than all of this was walking arm in arm with Altfor, the reality that he was her *husband*. The word filled her with a sense of dread. She felt, with every step she took, as if she were rejecting Royce. She told herself again and again that she was doing this for him. This was the path to power, she had to remind herself constantly, the only way to save Royce and her people. If she continued to resist, she would be of no use to anyone.

She understood it intellectually; yet in her heart, it was beyond painful to live with day in and day out. She hated pretending to be in love with someone else. It was contrary to everything she was, to the life she had led. Yet to save Royce, she saw no other way.

What was worse than all of this was that, as much as she hated to admit it, she did not feel entirely uncomfortable in Altfor's arms. As she settled into married life, she could not help notice how easy it was, how comfortable she felt, how kind Altfor was to her, how gentle his touch. He tried so hard to make her happy. He genuinely loved her.

That, too, was a funny feeling. She didn't *want* him to love her. She wanted him to hate her. That would make all this so much easier.

And while she did not love him, she also had to admit to herself that she did not hate him, either. There were much worse men in the world. And that feeling was what made her hate herself the most.

"Do you see this?" he asked.

She looked up, startled from her thoughts, to see him waving gently out to the land before them. She took in the vista, startled by its beauty. Here, at the end of the stone plaza, looking out along the western orchards, leaning against the marble railing, she saw the whole countryside spread out before her, a view she never tired of. She saw the rolling hills of Sevania, the sun shining down on glorious farms and vineyards. Fields of color bordered them, farmers tilling the soil, collecting the flowers.

She squinted and could just make out one of the distant villages dotting the landscape—hers—and the thought filled her with longing. She missed her people dearly. She missed her old, simple life. She would give up all of this in a heartbeat to be farming. These, the trappings of wealth, brought her no joy. Only freedom could bring her joy.

"It is all yours now," Altfor continued, turning to her with a satisfied smile. "I have been appointed by my father on this day as Duke of the Western lands. As my wife, you are Duchess, and you now own all of this land jointly with me. All you see before you, the Western lands, I am giving them all to you."

She looked back at him, stunned. With just a few words he had given her more land than her ancestors could have worked off in a lifetime.

"It is true," he said, smiling. "My father conferred the new title upon me this morning. I am the chosen son now. *I* am the one who will rule all of this."

He smiled as he gently pulled a strand of hair back from her face and ran his fingers along her cheek. She wished his fingers were not so smooth, his touch so loving. She wished she could feel repulsed by him. And she hated that she did not.

"You are my *wife*," he said. "Anything you want, anything you see, is now yours. That vineyard there; that orchard; those people's homes; that entire village. *Anything* you want. I can build a castle just for you. I can have the peasants mine the gold mines of Sevania, fashion you the finest jewels you've ever seen. It is a prosperous land we live in, and it is yours for the taking."

He smiled, clearly thinking she would be impressed.

Yet she felt only repulsion. She wanted none of it. Those lands he spoke of, as if they were his private playthings, were *her* lands, her people's lands. She had worked them with her bare hands, had helped make them what they were—not him. What gave him—or any of the nobles—the right to lay claim to any of it?

Inside, she fumed. But she forced herself to hold her tongue. She reminded herself that he meant only to express his love to her. He was ignorant of how she felt. And she knew that to fight with him now would do no good. She forced herself to remember what she really wanted: Royce, and her people, to be free.

"Tell me," he pressed. "What would you like?"

Genevieve took a deep breath, a long, slow, sad breath as she turned and studied the countryside. It was such a beautiful land, and such a shame that it was controlled by so few. She wanted the people down there to be free.

"I ask for one thing only," she finally said, her voice soft and gentle.

"Tell me, my love, what is it?" he said, pressing her hands. "Anything."

She took a deep breath.

"To give my family, and my village, back what is theirs. To allow them to own their own land and to no longer tithe to the nobles. They must give away most of what they have and they often go hungry. Especially the children. Just allow them to keep their own crops."

He blinked, clearly stunned.

"I should be surprised by your selfless request," he said, "yet I am not. It is in keeping with your nature. Your heart is truly pure. You are unlike anyone I've ever met."

He smiled and nodded.

"Your request shall be granted. Your people can keep whatever they want."

She felt a huge rush of relief. She marveled that she had just achieved more than an entire army could. Perhaps Moira had been right after all.

"And what about you?" he pressed. "What can I give *you*?"

She shook her head.

"I want nothing."

He clasped her hands.

"Surely, there must be one thing?" he pressed.

Suddenly, it came to her. There was one thing.

"There is," she said. "Royce's brothers. They remain in the dungeon. Yet they harmed no one. I would like them to be free."

Slowly, like a dark cloud moving in on a summer day, his face darkened.

"You still dream of him, don't you?" he asked, his voice dark. It came out as an accusation.

She looked away, hoping he would not see the expression on her face.

His face darkened even more, and after a long silence, his jaw clenched.

"No," he said, harshly.

With that single word he turned and strutted off. She could see how much she had angered him, and a new sense of dread filled her. She wondered what vengeful act he would take.

Would he have them killed?

Royce, she thought, as a tear fell from her cheek, studying the distant horizon, *come home to me.*

*

Genevieve walked quickly through the castle streets, on urgent business, the villagers all bowing their heads dutifully as she passed, as if she were royalty. She did not realize how elegant her dress was until she saw the faces of all these people getting out of her way, bowing, saying, "My lady," from every direction. It was not long ago when she would herself be the one to be hurrying out of a noble's way. It was unnerving to her. She wished they wouldn't look at her this way. She wished they would just accept her as one of their own, as they used to.

Genevieve walked quickly, trying to ignore all the attention, forcing herself to stay focused as she hurried to where she needed to go. As she thought of her destination, she felt a flurry of anxiety in her stomach. It might not go well. And it was very risky of her to even try.

She crossed the castle courtyard, bustling with people, horses, dogs, chickens, keeping her head lowered, trying to stay inconspicuous, until she passed through a low stone arch. She turned, passed through an open-air corridor, and stopped before a thick, oak door.

It was blocked by two royal guards, and they stared back, puzzled.

"My lady," they each said.

She nodded back, her heart pounding inside, trying to keep her cool as she stared back at the entrance to the dungeons.

"I have come to see Royce's brothers," she said.

They looked her over skeptically.

"On whose authority?" one asked.

"The Duke's," she lied.

A long, tense moment of silence followed. Her heart pounded, as she was flooded with anxiety. What if they denied her access? What if they told the Duke?

They exchanged another glance, then finally, to her immense relief, they stepped aside and opened the door. She breathed deep inside. Clearly her appearance, her dress and jewels, carried more authority than a letter from the King himself. It amazed her how people always judged on appearances.

Genevieve walked in, heart pounding, knowing each step was getting her deeper into trouble. She was, after all, defying the Duke's command. She could only hope that word would not reach him.

It was dim, cool, and damp in here, and Genevieve shuddered as she walked quickly down the bare stone corridors, escorted by one of the guards. He led her down a twisting set of spiral stairs, claustrophobic, getting darker as they went. Soon the only light to see by was from his flickering torch.

Genevieve could hear the squeal of rats in the darkness as they reached the lowest level. They marched down another stone corridor, until finally they came to a heavy iron gate. As they did, the guard marched away, leaving her facing two new guards.

They unlocked the cell and stepped aside and Genevieve entered, her heart breaking to think of Royce's brothers—who had been like brothers to her—down here. She walked slowly, cautiously, passing rows of cells, desperate faces staring back at her solemnly in the darkness.

Finally, she stopped before the final cell. She turned and peered into the darkness and there, her heart fell to see, were Royce's three brothers, all sitting on the stone floor, dejected. They looked back up at her like cornered animals, eyes wide with surprise—and all at once they stood and hurried across the cell.

"Genevieve!" Raymond exclaimed.

She could hear the relief in his voice, as he rushed forward and grabbed the bars, his brothers beside him, hope slowly creeping into their faces. Seeing them made her think of Royce, and she felt her heart tear with emotion. She felt hope for the first time since this ordeal had begun, yet she also felt a wave of guilt. She hated herself for not coming here sooner, but this was the first time she'd been afforded the leniency to travel freely.

"What has happened?" asked Raymond.

"Where's our brother?" asked Lofen.

"Is he safe?" asked Garet. "Have you heard anything?"

That was so like them. Here they were, sitting in a dungeon, and all they cared for was their brother's safety. It deepened Genevieve's sadness and made her hate herself even more. While these fine men were all suffering, she was enjoying the luxuries of living in the castle—and in the enemy's arms. The enemy they had risked their lives to free her from.

"I have heard nothing," she replied, a tear falling as she did.

Their faces fell with disappointment.

"I pray for him every day," she added. "And watch for him every night."

Raymond suddenly had a new look to his face as he slowly looked her up and down, recognizing her garb for the first time. A look of disapproval—and then of suspicion—crept over his face.

"And yet you wear the garb of the nobles," he said, his voice dark and hard.

The other brothers examined her, too, and she watched their faces drop with condemnation.

"Have you forgotten our brother so soon?" Garet asked.

Genevieve felt a pain in her chest at his words.

"I love your brother with all that I am," she said.

"And yet your dress says otherwise," Lofen replied. "Have you married one of them?"

They looked at her, aghast, and she did not know what to say.

"Had I a choice?" she finally replied. "I was taken, remember?"

"We remember very well," Raymond replied. "Our brother lost his life—we have all lost our lives—because of that day."

"What would you have me do?" she asked.

"To be taken is one thing," Lofen said. "To be wed is another."

She shook her head, trying to get the words out, unsure what to say. The problem was that she shared their feelings—she hated herself, too.

"It is not what you think," she finally said, trying to explain and not knowing where to begin.

Yet as she stood there she could see in their faces that their feelings were hardening. They were all beginning to hate her, their minds made up, and she could see that nothing she said would change their minds.

"I've come here to talk to you," she explained, in a rush. "To see if there is some way I can help you. To try to free you. To try to find a way to—"

"We want nothing from you," Raymond spat.

The venom in his tone hurt her heart.

"It is clear what you have become," he continued. "You've turned your back on Royce—and have become a traitor to us all."

"I have not!" she cried.

One by one they turned their backs on her and retreated to the far end of the cell. They would not look at her again.

Genevieve broke down weeping. She did not know what to say, how to explain herself. She wanted to tell them she would die for them, any of them. But the words would not come out, replaced only by sobs.

Genevieve slowly realized that nothing she could say would make any difference now. Coming here, she realized, had been a horrible mistake.

Unable to control her emotions, she turned and ran, weeping as she fled the dungeon, wondering if she could ever have her old life back again.

CHAPTER TWENTY NINE

Altfor rode out into the countryside, sword at his side, horse thundering beneath him. He rode with the fury that built up within him almost unstoppably at the thought of the things his wife had asked of him. This foolishness of kindness to peasants was almost a kind of betrayal; a proof that she hadn't put her old life behind her, even though he had plucked her out of the mire, made her his in law when he could simply have taken what he wanted from her.

He had promised her that he would not be his brother, and Altfor had meant it. Manfor had been a fool, with no understanding of the subtlety that had to accompany power. A noble could do what he wanted, of course, but even so, it paid to pick the right moment.

Altfor rode out toward his wife's former village in search of his moment.

She had tried to fool him, he was sure of it. She had asked for favors for the brothers of her former love. It was only one step from asking for mercy for him! Anger flared up in Altfor at the thought of that, and he rode harder, forcing his horse forward in spite of its complaints.

Finally, he found the village, staring down at a peasant child so grubby it was a wonder that it was permitted to keep living.

"I am looking for the family of Genevieve, who was taken from this village," he said. "I believe she has a sister named Sheila, and parents still living?"

The child, it was so filthy it was impossible to tell if it was a boy or a girl, looked up at him in fear.

Altfor half drew his sword. "An answer, or you're no use to me."

"That way," the child said, pointing. "The house with the blue flowers around the door."

Altfor rode on, looking for the house the child had described. Sure enough, there was a house with blue flowers marking it out from the others. He could have rode up to the door and forced his way inside, but that was the way his brother would have done things: obvious and foolish. He could do the same thing far more subtly.

When hunting, a fool charged in, while a true hunter enjoyed the stalking and the waiting, taking his time, savoring the moment.

Altfor waited, staying out of sight until a woman came out from the house. One glance, and it was obvious that she was Genevieve's sister, her looks the same, even her way of moving. She wasn't quite as beautiful as his wife, but this wasn't about that. This was about the fact that he could do it. He ruled here.

He followed her, walking his horse as he followed on the route to a nearby wood. The path grew rougher, the trees forming a canopy overhead, in drovers' paths that were empty so far from a market day.

There he saw her collecting plants a little way from the path. Altfor tethered his horse, moving with all the silence of a hunter stalking a doe. He approached from behind her, amusing himself with the thought that from this angle, she could almost be her sister.

"You're Sheila, aren't you?" he said gently as he grew close. "Genevieve's sister?"

He saw her start and spin toward him, caught between the urge to run and the surprise at being recognized.

"My... my lord," she stammered out. There was a hint of strength there, but nothing like that in his wife. A pity. Altfor would have enjoyed breaking it from her.

"Yes, I am your lord," he said. He smiled a predatory smile. "Did you know that your sister asked me to be kind to the peasantry?"

"N-no, my lord."

Altfor struck her then, mostly because he could. "Do not say no to me. Peasants do not get to say no to their lords, do they, wench?"

"N... as you say, my lord," she said.

He saw her glance back, and wondered if she would try to run. There was some thrill to be had in the chase, but control was more amusing.

"If you run, I'll catch you, and I'll kill you," he promised.

He saw her freeze in place. "What do you want?"

Altfor smiled at that. "Oh, all kinds of things. Do you know, there are things that a man is not meant to do with his wife, since she becomes a noble the moment that he marries her. There are things that are reckoned *demeaning* for a noble."

"I... did not know that," Sheila replied. He could see her looking for a way to run again.

"If you run, I'll kill you slowly," he said. "Oh, the things I would do to you. The things I *will* do to you. But you'll live. I find that most people will put up with almost anything to live. Peasants will eke out an existence, tolerate any cruelty, because the alternative is losing their lives."

She stood there trembling, and Altfor found himself a little disappointed. Genevieve would probably have had some defiant comeback.

"What about you?" he asked, leveling his sword. "What will you do to live?"

The girl hesitated, and Altfor could see the fear in her. He enjoyed it.

"Anything, my lord," she finally said. "I'll do anything."

Altfor smiled and put his blade to the fabric of her dress, feeling her trembling. He cut it away with a sharp yank.

"Yes," he assured her. "You will."

*

When he was done, Altfor left the girl bruised and whimpering on the leaf-littered floor of the wood. Let her stumble and stagger her way back; he didn't care. He made his way back to his horse, riding through the forest, feeling alive as he rarely did when he had to constrain himself with rules and propriety.

His brother had shared that, of course, except that Manfor had been a fool about it. Altfor thought more, planned more, and did not rush in when he could take his pleasures just as easily without the risks. He heeled his horse forward, increasing its speed to a gallop as he made his way back toward the castle.

There were attendants waiting for him, of course. They thronged around, desperate to impress for some hint of praise or recognition. Altfor ignored them, keeping his eye on the balcony where Genevieve and Moira stood talking. He considered how his wife would scream if he did half of what he'd done with her sister with her.

As it was, he would have to settle for a different sort of cruelty.

"My wife has asked that I be gentle with the brothers of the traitor Royce," he said. "Take them from the dungeons, take them to a place of execution, and have them hanged."

CHAPTER THIRTY

Royce walked off the plank and took a step onto dry land for the first time in weeks, and stopped, breathed deep, and smelled the air, smiling. He relished the feeling of being back on dry land, of having steady earth beneath him, of returning to his homeland. The voyage was over. He had made it.

It was a disorienting feeling at first to not have the earth moving beneath him, and he felt relieved and disturbed at the same time. He was relieved that he was finally off the ship, away from the Red Isle, back on the same continent as his family and Genevieve—yet disturbed because his arrival here only meant one thing: it was time for him to face the Pits.

Beside him, Mark, Altos, and Rubin stepped forward, the four of them standing side by side, surrounded by dozens of Empire soldiers who stepped up to greet them, new shackles in hand. Royce looked around and found they had docked in a small, teeming harbor village, led into a bustling crowd of villagers hurrying about their daily business. Within moments all four of them were already shackled, with nowhere to run.

Royce stood with the others in the small town square as dozens of curious villagers glanced at them askance. His homeland seemed much busier, faster, more crowded than when he had left it all those moons ago. Perhaps the emptiness, the quiet, of the Red Isle had seeped into him. The faces of all these people seemed to be those of strangers, and Royce hardly felt as if he had returned home.

They dragged him and the others through the village, to a large, open-air cage that was little better than the kind of thing they might have kept a bear or a wolf in before they baited it with dogs. There were other men in there, most of whom looked desperate and dangerous; hard men and thugs who didn't have anything left to lose. They hadn't trained on the Red Isle, though, and Royce found himself wondering how long they would truly last once the fighting started.

He and the others were thrown into the cage without preamble, and Royce looked around, making sure that none of the men there were going to attack. Most of them kept to themselves, heads down or staring out defiantly as if that would somehow fend off any danger. Royce found an empty spot in one corner, and the others sat with him, forming a kind of square with their eyes on the others there.

"One of us should stay awake at all times," Mark said.

Altos shrugged. "Do you think they'll really attack?"

"They might," Royce said. "Desperate men will do anything."

"Then what will *we* do?" Mark asked.

Royce didn't have an answer to that. He and the others had all the skills of the Red Isle, and as much reason to try to break free as anyone, yet there was no hope of doing anything now, not stuck inside the cage like this.

"We wait," he said. "We sleep, and we hope that it's enough."

A guard came past, close enough that Royce could have reached out and pulled him back against the bars if he'd tried.

"Look at you," the man said with a laugh. "The finest of the Red Isle? You're nothing more than a pack of whelps."

"If you think we're so weak," Royce said, "why not try your luck? Let me out of this cage, pass me a sword, and we'll see how you do."

For a moment, he thought that he'd caught the man's pride enough that he might actually do it, but no, the guard slammed the butt of his halberd against the bars instead, making Royce jump back.

"Mind how you speak to your betters, boy, or you'll find yourself whipped before you go in to fight. Not that it makes much difference. None of you will survive what happens tomorrow. I'll be watching comfortably from the side while you and your friends are gutted."

*

Genevieve saw Altfor's return through one of the windows of her chambers, and steeled herself, having to build up the layers of herself that served to disguise what she really felt. She held back all the distaste and the fear, replacing it with the façade of happiness, even love, that he would require of her.

"You shouldn't make it so obvious," Moira said.

"You're the one telling me to pretend to be what I'm not," Genevieve pointed out.

"But it doesn't work if people see that you're just pretending. If you go from hate to love so quickly, it's obvious that it's a mask." Moira shrugged and moved to the door. "Maybe Altfor won't notice. Ned is hardly bright."

Genevieve dismissed that idea straightaway. Altfor was many things, but he wasn't stupid. She would need to be more careful.

"You aren't staying?" Genevieve asked. Moira's presence would make things easier.

"I have things I have to do," she replied. "I'm sure you'll be fine."

She slipped out of the door before Genevieve could say anything else, and Genevieve sat there, trying to compose herself better. Moira was right; it was too suspicious if she was suddenly in love with a husband she had professed to hate.

Altfor looked... happy wasn't quite the right word. Satisfied, perhaps, with a look of hunger when he stared her way that made Genevieve's stomach tighten.

"Hello there, wife," he said, and Genevieve knew that had to be deliberate, reminding her that she was his, and had no choice in any of this. "I trust you have been well here?"

"Well enough," Genevieve said, taking Moira's advice and not quite disguising all that she felt. "Should I pretend to be happy for you?"

Altfor's expression hardened a touch. "You can pretend or not. It makes no difference to the fact that you are mine to do with as I wish."

Genevieve bit back her response to that, knowing that to argue was to make things harder for herself. Instead, she lowered her gaze, trying to appear demure.

"A pity that you couldn't be with me before," Altfor said. "The things you would have seen. I met your sister."

Genevieve felt her blood run cold as Altfor smiled. "My sister? What did you do?"

Altfor just kept smiling. "Merely catching up with my wife's family, letting her know how much I value you."

Genevieve stared at him, trying to work out exactly what happened and not daring to try to think of it.

"What did you *do?*" Genevieve demanded again.

Again, Altfor didn't answer directly. Instead, he took his time about going and pouring himself wine, sipping it as though enjoying her discomfort.

"Tell me, Altfor!"

He threw the glass at the wall, making Genevieve jump as it shattered.

"You do not give me commands. I give them to you, and you please me."

"But my sister..." Genevieve began.

"Your sister is a peasant and unmarried," Altfor said. "I have every right."

The full horror of what her husband had done hit Genevieve then.

"Why?" she asked.

"Every time you displease me, I will find a way to hurt you. Sometimes I will hurt you directly, and I'll enjoy that. Sometimes, I'll hurt the ones you claim to love, to remind you that you are mine."

"No," Genevieve said, feeling the tears that had started to pour from her eyes, and wanting to hold them back so that he wouldn't see them. "No."

Altfor seemed to be enjoying her misery. "I know that you're disappointed at missing out on the moment. Still, perhaps tomorrow we can have a moment together when we visit the Pits."

Genevieve wasn't sure what to say to that. There was only one thing she could think of Altfor dragging her to see the fighting for, and it was just about the only thing that could make that moment worse.

"Royce? You're taking me to see Royce fight, aren't you?"

"I'm taking you to see him die," Altfor said.

Genevieve shook her head. She knew that she was supposed to pretend that she was happy with Altfor, supposed to be the person he expected, but right then the horror of it all was almost overwhelming.

"No, I won't," she said.

Altfor was on her in an instant, his hand balled in her hair. "You will do exactly as you are told. You get no choice in it."

"You can't make me," Genevieve said.

"I can make you do whatever I want. Currently, I have no plans to visit your sister again. Currently, your sister lives. Would you like that to change?"

Genevieve tried to look away, but he wouldn't let her.

"So, you *do* have a choice. Will you come tomorrow to the pits, or the day after so that we can watch your sister die?"

She bit her lip, unable to speak.

Altfor tossed her away.

"I'm glad that's settled. Now, when I get back, be ready for bed. And this time, pretend better that you love me, or I'll think of another way to punish you."

CHAPTER THIRTY ONE

Royce felt the cold metal of new shackles on his wrists, and he knew he was at a crossroads. The apprehension in his stomach deepened as he looked at his friends' faces staring back and knew that this was very likely the last time he would see them alive.

Mark stepped forward and managed to reach out a hand, and clasped Royce's arm before the soldiers could yank him away.

"You've been a good friend," Mark said. "I hope to one day repay the favor."

Royce thought of all they had been through, and he could only nod as he clasped his friend's arm.

"You already have," Royce replied.

Altos clasped his arm.

"Do not forget me," he said meaningfully.

And then, to Royce's surprise, Rubin stepped up too, clasping his arm before he was yanked away. He nodded sadly, and Royce could see in his face a look of respect, one he'd never expected to see from him.

"I am good to my word," Rubin called out. "I shall repay my debt to you."

Royce found himself yanked roughly by the shackles, pulled forward into the crowd. At the same moment, a leather mask was pulled down roughly over his face, leaving slits for eyes and slits to breathe, but disguising him otherwise. This was, he realized, how they adorned the fighters in the Pits.

Royce was soon led through chaotic village. Shouts and cheers rose up as a crowd began to take notice and thicken around him. They all peered at him as if he were an animal in a zoo, paraded through the town. He did not like the feeling. Some villagers patted him on the back, while others taunted him.

Royce understood the crowd's reaction. Most of those thrown into the Pits, he realized, were hardened criminals, there for murder or worse crimes. They assumed he was the same. If only they knew, Royce thought, that he was there for no other reason than for attempting to retrieve his stolen bride. Would they greet him like this then?

Royce was pushed and shoved down the center of the village, while the cries of the crowd reached a deafening point. He felt something building, as if he were being led somewhere.

Finally they stopped short, and as the crowd parted ways, Royce stopped and looked down in shock at the sight before him.

There, at his feet, was a massive pit, twenty feet in diameter, twenty feet deep. At its edge stood hundreds of spectators, cheering as he walked forward.

They made him wait at the side of the pit, his shackles locked into place on a ring of iron there, while the fighting began.

Royce watched as they threw Altos down into the pit, and a trio of foes stood in front of him. He recognized all of them from the cages. All carried long knives that should have been no match for Altos's sword, but as they spread out around him, Royce could see the danger that his friend was in.

He was surrounded by them then, like an animal hemmed in by wolves, with no way to strike at one without being slain by the others. Worse, Royce had the feeling that he didn't even want to *try* to fight back in that moment. He stood there, sword down, staring up at Royce and the others, while the three men closed in.

In that moment, he could have sprung forward to fight, could have struck at them, could have *fought*. Instead, he just stood there as the first of the men stabbed him in the back with a long knife.

Another slashed across his throat, and the third hung back, as if expecting Altos to still have the strength to kill even now. Royce had to kneel there, watching his friend die, braver in death than he thought he ever could be.

The crowd booed the moment, clearly expecting more.

"This is what they pay good money to the Red Isle for?" one of the guards muttered. "They're supposed to be *better* for all that training."

"Maybe if we're so weak," Rubin said, "you'd like to kill us yourself?"

"Or maybe I just need to throw in more than one of you, and give the crowd a proper show," the guard countered. He and the others with him unchained Rubin and Mark, flinging them down into the pit, tossing their weapons after them.

"What about me?" Royce demanded. If he had to die, he wanted to do it standing side by side with his friends, and maybe, just maybe, the three of them together would be able to find a way to fight their way out of this.

"Two of you are enough," the guard shot back, cuffing Royce at the side of the head and leaving him in place. "Let's see if your friends fight, or if they die like cowards too."

Mark and Rubin fought. Oh, how they fought. On the Red Isle, they hadn't liked one another, but now Royce saw them clasp hands briefly, then leap at the three convicts. The fight was so brief that Royce suspected that the crowd didn't have time to understand the skill that his friends showed. Mark feinted at one foe, then went for another, letting Rubin leap into the gap in the defenses that his feint had exposed. Rubin's sword flashed around the convict's guard, cutting deep into the artery of the leg, while Mark thrust his blade through the chest of another man. Both spun in time to face the third, Mark catching his blade while Rubin thrust up and under his ribs.

The crowd cheered, although Royce knew it was the blood they were cheering, not his friends.

"The old man next," the guard snapped.

"Wait, you're making them fight again?" Royce demanded.

The guard glowered at him. "You're here to die, boy, not to enjoy some glittering life. Your friends will fight and keep fighting until either the crowds are bored, they die, or we run out of foes for them. Now be quiet."

Royce sat there angrily, hoping that his friends would somehow find a way through this. He almost breathed a sigh of relief as he saw their next foe: an old man who didn't even wear the mask of a fighter, his white hair instead sticking up from an uncovered face. He *did* wear battered armor, though, that looked as though it had seen plenty of use, and carried a sword in two hands, the tip dragging along the ground. He stood in front of Mark and Rubin as if waiting for the moment when they would attack.

Then they did, tentatively, as if not quite believing that this old man was a threat. That caution was all that saved them in that first rush, the longsword their foe held sweeping around in murderous arcs, one scoring a line of blood across Mark's arm.

"Used to be a champion of one of the local lords, he did," the guard said in response to Royce's shocked look. "Killed the wrong man's son, though."

The old man certainly seemed to move with the deadliness of long practice. Mark and Rubin tried to circle him, but every time they seemed to have the man between them, he attacked one or the other, repositioning himself carefully.

He seemed to be getting tired though, his steps becoming more shuffling as the fight went on. He seemed to stumble for a moment, missing a step on the dirt floor of the pit. Royce saw the trap in it, and tried to cry out, but there was no way that his friends could hear him above the yells of the crowd.

Mark moved forward into the opening, swinging his sword down toward the older man, only to find it clattering off his armor. Royce saw his friend freeze in place as the old man thrust his sword up for Mark's chest.

Mark swerved, enough to miss its being a mortal blow.

But not enough to avoid serious injury.

The sword punctured his side, just barely. It could have been worse—but it could have been much better, too.

Mark dropped to the ground, unmoving, and it looked doubtful he would rise again.

Royce gasped, feeling the air leave his body.

There lay his best friend in the world, defeated already.

If you die, I die.

The words rang in his head.

In that moment, Royce felt as if *he* were the one being stabbed. "*No.*"

Rubin stabbed at the old man in a fury of blade work. Most of the blows bounced off the armor, but some got through. The knight managed to spin though, striking out with a dagger. Royce saw blood spurt, and in the seconds that followed, three bodies lay on the floor of the pit.

In the moments that followed, the crowd roared.

Royce sat there, feeling a mixture of disgust and horror at what was happening. He couldn't believe that at least one of his friends had been killed, and possibly the other, just like that. Royce felt numb, unable to believe the sheer waste of it.

"Mark!" he shrieked.

But his friend did not move.

The guard smirked at him. "Looks as though you're in luck, boy. You get to live a little longer. Let's get you back to your cage while we find more for you to face."

Royce wanted to scream at him, wanted to fight him. Wanted to kill him. Caught in chains as he was though, he couldn't even begin to do it. The guard and others with him dragged him back into the square, to the spot where the cage stood. They threw him back inside, leaving him there with the thugs and the criminals.

How long would it be before they came for him again? Were they even now trying to find things that might kill him? Royce looked around the cage, wondering why the men there hadn't been thrown in there against him. Maybe after the way Rubin and Mark had fought, they were worried that the men wouldn't be dangerous enough.

Royce settled down in the corner of the cage, trying to sleep, knowing that he would need all the rest he could get to have a chance to survive.

CHAPTER THIRTY TWO

Genevieve wandered the halls of the castle, looking for her husband even as she knew that this wasn't a moment that she wanted to speed up. She didn't want to rush in the moment when she would have to go to the Pits to see the violence of them. She *certainly* didn't want to move forward the moment when they would send Royce out to die.

She also didn't want to think about what Altfor might be doing while she delayed, though, not after the threats that he had made. What if the reason she couldn't find him was that he was out riding, heading closer to her sister by the moment? The thought of it made Genevieve sick.

"Where is my husband?" she asked one of the servants she passed. It was hard to think of the woman as her servant. She was her husband's, just as the castle was. Genevieve was his property, rather than his duchess.

She saw the servant hesitate, and fear filled her. "Where is he?"

This time, the servant pointed to a room a little way away. It was a room Genevieve recognized, because it belonged to just about the one person in the castle she trusted: Moira.

Genevieve ran across the space between her and the door, thinking that if Altfor was prepared to hurt her sister to get to her, then he wouldn't hesitate to harm her friend too, even if she was married to one of his brothers.

"Oh… Altfor!"

The sounds coming from the room didn't sound like those of pain though. They didn't sound like some furious fight, or even a quiet submission, forced upon Moira because there was no other option. Genevieve found her furious need to protect her friend replaced by simple fury, and she burst through a door that she half suspected had been left unlocked deliberately.

She saw them there then, tangled on Moira's bed: her friend and her husband, wrapped only in the sheets tangled around them, and Genevieve could only give thanks that they seemed to have rolled apart from one another in the moments when she was busy opening the door.

"Moira?" she said, unable to keep the hurt out of her voice. "How *could* you?"

She didn't ask it of her husband, even though he was the one sworn to her. She asked it of her friend; of the woman who'd *said* she was her friend. Then Moira smiled, and Genevieve saw that she had never been her friend at all.

"I *told* you that this was a place where you had to learn to pretend," Moira said, while Genevieve felt her heart starting to break. "And you have told me *so* many things that you wouldn't have told an enemy."

That was what she was, Genevieve realized. As fast as that, and the woman she had thought of as her closest friend was her enemy. Had she been meant to find Moira and Altfor like this? If so, which of them had decided that it was a good idea? Had it been her former friend, deciding that the moment was right to reveal her deception, or her cruel husband, finding one more way to harm her?

"I'll—" Genevieve began, starting forward.

Altfor caught her arm as she raised it. "You will do nothing. You will *say* nothing. You will go to the hall and wait for me, so that we can go to watch your dear Royce end his days."

Genevieve started to shake her head, but Altfor caught hold of her jaw with his other hand. He pressed a kiss on her, hard enough that it hurt.

"Go now, or I'll decide that you want to join us. And be ready when I want to go. If I have to come looking for you, you won't like it."

Genevieve ran from the room, not daring to look back.

CHAPTER THIRTY THREE

Dust walked into the village, unmoved by its poverty, its dirt, its sense that it was only one bad harvest away from being a place of ghosts. To him, everywhere held ghosts, and today was a day for making more. That much was foreseen.

"There is a boy from here," he said to the first man he met, "with a mark on his arm."

"You think I've got time to stop and talk to every stranger I meet?" the man demanded. "I've geese to go to market."

He started forward, and Dust stepped into his path.

"Out of the way," the man said, extending an arm as if he might brush Dust aside. Dust grabbed the arm and broke it as easily as he might have broken a twig, ignoring the man's screams.

"I have learned many things," Dust said. "I have learned ways of bringing death from a hundred tomes. I have learned to step in silence and to sit patient as a stone without eating for days. I have learned to read the signs in all things. Those signs have led here. I will ask one more time. Where is the boy with the mark on his arm?"

"You mean Royce?" the man managed, between pained breaths. "His family... his family live on the farm at the edge of the village. That way."

"Thank you," Dust said, and set off through the village. People were staring at him now, and he guessed that for once it had to do with more than his gray skin. A group of men were gathering, farm tools in their hands. He wondered if they knew anything of the signs that could be read in crowds, the way a man could read their intentions. Probably not, or they would know how obvious the anger building up in them was. They would stand there until one gained the courage to strike, and then they would all act.

Dust could see which one, too, the signs pointing to a man holding a scythe as if it were a true weapon. He was the largest man there, and clearly one used to fighting. Once he struck, the others would descend, but then, the opposite was true as well.

Dust stepped forward in the space between two heartbeats, gripping the scythe firmly and twisting, ripping it from the other man's grasp as easily as he might have from a child. He took a moment to learn the weight of the weapon, and perhaps his masters would have disapproved of that, for a man like him should know the way of death in all things.

He made up for it in the next moment though, when he spun and swept it across the man's throat in a whisper of metal. He stepped back, avoiding the blood that fountained; people never understood how much there could be in a body. He shouldered the scythe like a spear, continuing to walk.

People fell back from him then, some yelling, some simply screaming. Dust let them. How could they know that he had just let them live, killing the one person who mattered? He continued on toward the farm, reaching it and looking around for signs that it was the right place.

A solitary magpie sat above the door. The moss on the lintel had grown into the shape of something that might have been one of the *enatharis* symbols. That was a sign of a different sort.

Dust set the scythe down patiently by the door, then kicked the door, hard enough to splinter it as it broke open.

Two figures, a man and a woman, sat within, rising from their seats far too slowly. Dust raised a hand in warning.

"Stop," he said. "I have no wish to kill you."

His words were enough to slow them, at least.

"Where is your son?" he asked.

The man looked as though he might try to fight, and in that moment, Dust wished that he had gotten some blood on him before, since that might intimidate a man like this more. Instead, he held out his hands in a gesture of peace.

"I have no wish to fight you. Where is your son?"

"Which son?" the woman demanded in a sob. "Royce was taken away to the Red Isle to be given over to die in the Pits. Our other sons… the Duke threw them in a dungeon, and he'll kill them when he can."

Dust could understand how it must feel for her. His studies had shown him that most people found death distressing. His masters had even made him learn the death rituals of a hundred places, things that were meant to soothe or reconcile, bring completion to the living as well as the dead.

Still, he had a task.

"Which son has a mark on his arm?" he asked. "The seers who sent me spoke of only one boy."

"What do you want with Royce?" the man asked.

"He has a dangerous destiny," Dust said, seeing no reason to lie. "I have been sent to kill him."

"You… is this some kind of joke?" the man said. He lunged for a spot in the hovel, coming up with a sword. "You think I'm going to let you hurt my boy?"

Dust gave a short bow. "Forgive me, but you cannot stop me. You both die here today."

"I thought you said you didn't want to kill us," the woman said.

"I do not," Dust said. He looked around in case there was another sign to countermand the ones he'd seen, but there was nothing. "There was a death sign above your door, though, and I must act as fate requires."

"You're a monster," the woman said.

The man was more direct. He lunged at Dust, and Dust swayed aside, ignoring the blade as he struck at the man's throat, his fingers shattering cartilage and rending into bone. He stepped back to let the man collapse. A body without air was a dead body.

He stepped over to the woman, cradling her head almost gently, ignoring her screams.

"I will say a prayer over your body," he promised, "and commend it to death. Then I will find your son. If it is any comfort, even some of the sages feel that people may be reunited after death, so perhaps you will see him."

She continued to scream, and it was a sound Dust had always found unpleasant. It did no good, so why do it? He twisted sharply, breaking her neck and stopping her wailing. He laid her down and started to say one of the shorter prayers for the dead that he knew. He had so much to do that there was no time for more.

Their son had gone to the Pits.

And that was where he must go.

CHAPTER THIRTY FOUR

Royce dreamed of a place that he had never been, standing above a battle where it seemed that a hundred thousand people clashed together in steel and wood and violence. He was standing above it all, next to a tree that had clearly been blackened by fire. A man stood there in white armor that covered him from head to toe, as tall and proud as the tree had probably once been. Royce knew without being told who he had to be.

"Father?"

The white-armored knight turned to him. "And you are Royce, the boy who was destined."

"I don't understand," Royce admitted.

"Do you see below?"

Royce watched the seemingly endless clash of the armies there. There were men there dressed after the fashion of knights, and others dressed in stranger, older ways, from the scale armor of the kingdom's first settlers, to men who seemed to wear little more than paint scrawled into protective talismans as they fought.

"I see them," Royce said.

"All of them scrambled in their time over who was the strongest, or the fastest, or the finest. All of them wanted to be a king because they thought they could use their strength to control others. You, though... you truly *are* as strong as they think they are. You will be the finest of us."

"I..." Royce didn't know what to say to that. "How, when I'm about to be thrown into the Pits to die alone?"

"Do you think you're alone when all of these are here behind you?" his father said. "I will be there with you. You have a great destiny before you."

"What destiny?" Royce demanded. "What am I meant to do?"

There was no answer, though, beyond a hammering in his ribs that seemed to go beyond any of the clashes of steel in that place. Royce found that hammering pulling at him, while the yells and screams of the warriors below seemed to resolve themselves into a different kind of yelling...

"...wake up or I'll whip you until you do," the guard snapped, aiming another kick at Royce. Royce was quick enough to avoid it, coming up to his feet smoothly, and maybe the grace with which he did it was enough to make the man reconsider yet another blow. Instead, the guard smiled nastily.

"It's your turn, boy. All the fine folk will be there to watch you die."

He and the guards took Royce out again, sliding the mask of the Pit fighters into place once more. Royce walked through the village as he had the first time, hearing the cheers and boos of the crowd around the Pit.

His dream hung on him like a cloud. He wondered if it was real—or just some hopeful figment of his imagination.

He came to a halt in the same spot as before. Before he even had a chance to process it all, Royce heard a clinking, then felt his shackles being unlocked.

He looked everywhere for Mark, praying he was still alive somewhere.

"Is Mark alive?"

But Royce was shoved forward.

He was airborne. His stomach dropped as he fell through the air, falling a good twenty feet until he landed on the muddy ground below, winded.

The crowd roared, and Royce scrambled to his feet, disoriented, his body covered in mud. He tried to quickly get his bearings. He looked up and saw at once that the walls were too steep and muddy to climb. Even if he could, up above the pit was ringed with hundreds of people, leaning over with pitchforks, clearly eager to prod him back down. It was a deathtrap.

Royce looked around, heart pounding, wondering why he was alone down there—when suddenly, the crowd erupted. He looked up and saw a blur of motion as something suddenly got shoved over the side. The crowd went wild as it landed in the pit, opposite Royce.

Royce stared in shock. He expected to see another fighter. But it was no fighter at all.

There, hardly twenty feet in front of him, was a monster. It resembled a tiger, but had two heads, long fangs, and long claws. It snarled as it stared back at him with angry red eyes.

Royce heard the frenzied clanging of metal, and he looked up to see the villagers frantically exchanging sacks of gold, betting on his fate.

The beast raised its head, bared its fangs, and roared, clearly preparing to pounce. Royce backed up, but his back soon hit the mud wall. There was no way out.

Defenseless, Royce braced himself as the monster leapt.

Heart slamming, nowhere to go, Royce felt his instincts kick in. He dropped to one knee, remembering his training, remembering the lessons Voyt had ingrained in him:

Use the foe's strengths as weaknesses.

Use the foe's size.

Use their lack of speed.

Do not hesitate.

Royce had been trained for this. He remembered the days he and his brothers had been thrown in a pit, pitted against animals, monsters, everything under the sun.

He focused. He curled himself in a ball, raised his hands overhead, and as the monster leapt, he shoved it in its soft belly, pushing with all his might, standing while he did so.

He threw the beast overhead, and it went flying through the air and slammed against the mud wall.

The crowd roared.

It landed on its feet, though, quicker than Royce had expected, and turned and faced him again. Royce knew that without a weapon, his options were limited. He was defenseless, after all, and there was nowhere to run. He might fend it off, but he could not win.

Perhaps, though, he could tire it out.

Use its own strength against it.

Royce searched the pit frantically and spied roots on the far side of the mud wall. He sprinted across the pit, and as the beast lunged at him again, he darted for them and leapt.

Royce grabbed one of the roots and with all his might pulled himself up. Soon he was up off the ground, four, five, six feet. He prayed that it held.

The monster lunged for him, and as it did, Royce curled into a bull, raising his feet. The beast just missed, grazing his foot, and slammed into the mud wall.

The crowd roared, clearly not expecting Royce to survive that.

Royce clung to the vine, climbing even higher, and as the furious beast snarled, the crowd cheered his ingenuity. Soon he was safely out of range.

Royce's heart pounded as he looked down, breathing hard, glad for the respite, wondering how he could ever win this. He looked up and saw the vine did not go very high, and he knew he could not climb to the top anyway, not with all the villagers waiting to prod him back down.

No sooner had he had the thought than there suddenly came an awful creaking noise—and he felt the worst feeling of his life: the root was slowly separating from the mud wall. Royce began to fall—and there was no way to stop it.

CHAPTER THIRTY FIVE

Raymond and his brothers were surviving the dungeon, but increasingly, it felt as though they weren't even close to it. Hunger gnawed at Raymond every second of the day, even though the three working together were able to grab their share of the bread whenever the guards remembered to throw it through. Pain rattled through his body from the fights that filled the place, while his mind... his mind couldn't ignore the screams that came from some of the shadows.

"The cart's out there again," Lofen said, standing on Garet's shoulders to look out of the window.

"Let me see," Raymond replied, as if it made any difference whether he saw it or not. Even so, his brother got down to let him up, and he clambered into place.

Sure enough, the execution cart stood there, ready to drag off some other poor soul to their death; or if not their death, then at least to something so bad that no one ever came back from it. How many people had they seen dragged out of the cells now, with no order to it and no sense? Sometimes it was the people who seemed to have been there longest; sometimes the ones who had only just arrived. Sometimes it was the ones who were most broken, sometimes the ones who still seemed to have a semblance of who they had been in the outside world.

Raymond jumped down heavily. Of his brothers, Lofen thought that the lack of a pattern was some kind of subtle torture, while Garet suspected that there was actually some subtle scheme to it that they simply couldn't detect. For his part, Raymond suspected that it was just about when the rulers of the place remembered those there and decided on a final punishment for them.

It wasn't a comforting thought as the door started to creak back against the wall.

"We need to be ready to fight our way out," Raymond whispered.

"Why?" Lofen replied. "I thought we were better not attracting attention."

"Like we can avoid it," Garet said.

"Quiet down there!" one of the guards who came in yelled. "Everyone back against the walls!"

Raymond backed up, as he had before when they'd come for others. He and his brothers kept to the shadows, and kept their silence. There were too many guards to risk anything else, and they were too weak by now to risk—

"You three!" the guard snapped, pointing with his club. Raymond's heart sank as he saw it pointed straight at him. "Looks as though your time is up. Orders of the Duke."

"No," Raymond said, trying to think, trying to come up with some way that he and his brothers could get out of this.

"Yes," the guard said. "Now come forward, or we come and get you."

Raymond looked around at the other prisoners, and even he didn't know why he did it. There was no help there. There had been none when he'd been one of the ones hanging back. In desperation, he lunged at the guard, figuring that at least dying in an honest fight would be better than whatever they had in store. He saw Lofen and Garet lunging with him, and wondered what might have happened if they'd been able to persuade the other prisoners to work with them; if that place hadn't bred so much mistrust that they would never work together.

As it was, Raymond felt the blunt impact of one club, then another. One caught him deep in the stomach, and he doubled over, trying not to vomit. Another slammed across his shoulder blades. The blows kept coming, and Raymond heard his own voice begging for it to stop.

Finally, it did, with his hands wrenched behind his back, rough chains used to hold his wrists.

"Up," the guard who seemed to be in charge ordered, "and be grateful I'd rather see you die at your appointed place!"

Raymond managed to stand, and saw his brothers struggling to do the same. The guards dragged them from the cell, and after so long down in the dark of the dungeon, the light made his eyes stream with tears. At least, Raymond wanted to think that it was the light.

The guards dragged them in the direction of the cart, and Raymond didn't even have the strength left to walk now, so they truly dragged him, feet scraping along the ground before they threw him into the back.

"Going to beg for your lives, boys?" the lead guard demanded, as he hopped into the driver's seat. Another guard jumped up beside him. "No? They all do eventually, you know, even the tough ones. Oh, the things they promise. Not that it makes any difference."

He made a clicking sound with his tongue, and the horse pulling the cart moved forward with the ponderous lack of effort that came with long practice. Raymond was happy for it to take as long as it wanted to then, because only one thing waited once it was done:

Death.

CHAPTER THIRTY SIX

Royce went flying through the air, landing back in the pit, just feet from the creature. The crowd cheered. No sooner had he landed than the beast landed on top of him, clawing and scratching furiously. Royce felt in awful pain from the blows, and he raised his bloody hands, trying to fend it off.

Royce knew he had but moments if he were to survive this. He reached up, desperate, and grabbed the beast by the throat. He spun and slammed it down, climbing on top of it. He squeezed, holding the beast just far enough away so that its claws missed him.

He squeezed and squeezed, choking the life out of it. Royce hated to hurt this beast, even if it was trying to kill him. But he knew if he did not, his life would be over.

Royce held on, even while the beast let out terrible snarls, writhing to kill him. But no matter what it did, Royce would not let go. He knew that to do so would mean his death.

Finally, the beast went limp in his arms.

Dead.

The thought both shocked and saddened Royce. He was relieved to kill it, but also sad to kill it.

The crowd fell silent, clearly stunned itself.

Royce rose to his feet, out of breath, covered in scratches and wounds, dripping blood. He was exhausted, and had no idea how he had won the match. His adrenaline had taken over in a wild blur.

It didn't matter. He had won. The deed was done and he had done what he had never wanted to: survive, at any cost.

Royce stood, half hoping that they might lower a rope, but knowing the truth of it too. He had seen what had happened to Mark and Rubin, had heard what the guard had said: he would fight on, again and again, until he either died or they grew bored. The cheers came again, growing louder, and Royce realized, with a sinking feeling, that his fighting had not even begun.

A fighter was suddenly thrown over the edge, landing in the pit but a few feet away from him, to the roaring of the crowd. Royce studied him. It was a huge man, muscular, wearing no armor or clothing whatsoever except for a loincloth and a sinister black mask covering his face. This man, with olive skin, covered in scars and tattoos, was clearly a professional killer.

The crowd cheered.

Royce backed up as the man came slowly, menacingly, toward him, a huge hatchet in his hand. Royce's heart sank. He did not see how he could escape this one.

Something came flying through the air, and as Royce heard it hit the mud beside him, he turned and was relieved to see what it was: a sword. *His* sword. The Crystal Sword.

Royce lunged and grabbed it, ducking from under the swing of the hatchet as it came down for his head.

The villagers roared as Royce raised the sword from the mud and faced his attacker. No sooner had he spun than his opponent came down at him with an awful shriek, raising the hatchet with both hands as if to split Royce in half. Royce raised his sword and blocked it, sparks flying everywhere, barely able to hold back the man's enormous strength, stopping the hatchet but inches from his face.

But his attacker, so fast, sidestepped in the same motion and head-butted Royce in the face, knocking him back several feet and onto his back.

Royce, sitting in the mud, was dizzy from the pain as the crowd roared. He looked up just in time to find the hatchet coming down for him again, and it barely missed him as he dodged. He then dodged the other way as the hatchet came down again. The man was incredibly fast.

This time the hatchet came straight down the middle. Royce, thinking fast, leaned back, spun around in the mud and swept the man's legs out from under him. His hatchet went flying.

The crowd roared, clearly surprised, as his foe now lay there, defenseless.

Royce regained his feet quickly and stood over him. As his foe scrambled in the mud, Royce knew this was his moment. He knew he had the power of death before him. This was his chance to kill his foe and be done with it and emerge the victor.

Yet as he stood over him, clenching his sword, he did not attack. Instead, he turned to the crowd, looked up, raised his sword for all the masses to see, and in full view of them all, he dropped it down to the mud. He would not let them control him. He would not kill an innocent man. He would not become the monster they wanted him to be.

Enraged, the crowd booed and hissed. In this one moment Royce had taken away their power. There was nothing they could do. They could not make Royce kill him. It was the one thing they did not have power over.

"I shall not kill a man for your pleasure!" Royce called out.

The crowd booed and hissed.

Royce turned and held his arms out, defenseless, as the man rose and faced him. The man stared back, clearly stunned for a moment,

"I shall not harm you," Royce said to his foe. "We are both slaves, controlled by the same system. Choose not to fight, and there will be nothing they can do. We will have triumphed over them."

Royce expected his foe to be grateful. Grateful that Royce had spared his life. Grateful that he was giving him a way to walk away.

But, to Royce's surprise, his foe scowled, clearly sharing no such sentiment. Ignoring Royce's entreaty, he reached down, grabbed his hatchet from the mud, and charged.

The crowd went wild.

Royce, defenseless, thought quick. He waited till the last moment then dodged out of the way. His foe charged past, stumbling, and Royce spun and kicked him in the kidneys as he did, sending him to the mud.

The crowd roared.

The man regained his feet and swung around quickly with his hatchet. Royce had not expected that; he jumped out of the way, yet still, the hatchet managed to graze his arm. It was enough to draw blood—and it hurt.

The crowd roared.

His foe threw his hatchet down and charged and suddenly tackled Royce, driving him down into the mud. Royce gasped as he hit the ground hard and they slid back several feet. Before he could get his bearings, the man, atop him, punched him in the face once, then twice, then three times.

Royce was dazed. This man meant to kill him, he could see it in his eyes. Indeed, he reached out with two hands, and Royce knew he meant to gouge his eyes out.

Royce grabbed the man's wrists on the way down, and his whole body shook from the effort. They were strong, broad, murderous wrists and were aimed directly for Royce's face.

The man's hands lowered, and Royce knew that in a few moments, it would all be over. This man would kill him.

The crowd cheered, egging him on, desperate for blood.

Suddenly, Royce felt his gaze blur before him, felt the world go still. The world melted away, and all fell silent. He strength rose within him. He felt himself succumb to a fresh rage, and he felt bigger than the universe.

Royce suddenly pushed the man's wrists upward, reversing the descent. He pushed more and more, until he found himself sitting up.

The man stared back, arms shaking, clearly shocked. Royce jerked his arms and threw his foe sideways.

The man tumbled in the mud, as Royce rose to his feet. The crowd cheered, ecstatic at this unexpected turn.

The man picked up his hatchet and came again, but this time, it was different. As he swung, Royce easily ducked and dodged every strike, again and again, the hatchet whistling past, Royce able to anticipate his every move. Finally, when he'd had enough, Royce stepped forward and kicked the heaving man in the chest, knocking him flat on his back and disarming him once again. He then retrieved his sword.

The crowd went wild as Royce stood over his foe, one foot on his chest, pinning him down.

The man looked up, dazed, humbled. For the first time, Royce saw fear in his eyes.

"Do it," the man said, blood trickling from his mouth.

Royce shook his head.

"I shall not."

Finally, the man nodded.

"I concede!" he called out.

The crowd booed and hissed.

"Kill him, kill him, kill him!" they chanted to Royce.

Royce dropped his sword and turned and looked up.

"*You* have lost!" he called up. "All of you have lost!"

Barely had he uttered the words than Royce heard a sudden grunting behind him; he spun at the last second to see his foe had retrieved his hatchet and was swinging it straight down for his head, aiming to chop him in half.

Royce dodged the blow and rolled. He snatched up the sword by instinct and swung it at head height.

The crowd roared as his foe's head fell clear.

Royce looked down at his foe's dead body, never having felt so sick.

A rope was lowered for Royce's ascent, and sheathing his sword, he grabbed it and pulled himself up, one foot at a time.

As he reached the top, he felt the hands of the villagers patting his back, uttering his name again and again. He stood there in an altered state, feeling his life spinning before him.

"ROYCE! ROYCE! ROYCE!"

Yet in his daze, three things came into focus. The first was the man presiding over the Pits. A noble, dressed in royal purple. Royce recognized him immediately: he was the local lord who had sentenced him to the Pits. Manfor's father. Lord Nors.

The second was this noble's son, standing there beside him, in his fineries, wearing the emblem of a duke, a haughty, arrogant look upon his face.

And the third, to his utter horror, was Genevieve. There she was. Dressed in royal garb, just like them.

Arm in arm with the duke.

Royce stood there, numb with horror. Genevieve was looking back at him, but she did not, he realized, recognize him. Of course—he was still wearing his mask.

Slowly, Royce lifted the mask covering his face, and as he did, he stared right back at her.

Genevieve's eyes widened and she stopped, frozen, and stared back at him. He could see the shock on her face. Clearly, she had not expected to see him there, either. She seemed too stunned to utter a word.

Everything inside Royce died at once. How could it be possible? There was his beloved, the girl he had risked it all for, the girl he had grown up with, standing there, arm in arm with a noble. After all of this, she had betrayed him.

Royce's heart shattered. He felt so much pain that he didn't know what to do with it.

More than that, he felt ire, a desire for vengeance against these nobles who had created these pits, who had put all these brave warriors in this awful position. Someone had to do something. Someone had to put an end to it now.

Royce reached over, snatched a spear from a villager's hand, and hurled it with all his might.

It soared through the air, straight and true, and before anyone in the stunned crowd could react, it found a spot in Lord Nors's chest. Fitting, Royce thought. After all, he was the man who had sentenced him, the man who had started it all.

Lord Nors gasped, holding it with both hands, then keeled over and died on the spot. Royce did not give the crowd time to react. He turned and bolted into the masses.

A horn sounded, and dozens of soldiers pursued. He could hear them behind him, gaining speed. But Royce had a head start—and he was fast. His power overcame him, and he outran them all. He spotted a horse, hopped onto it, and after a firm kick he was galloping, leaving this muddy village, heading out into the open countryside, far, far from this place.

He looked back one last time, despite himself.

And the last thing he saw, before he disappeared for good, was Genevieve's face, staring back at him, the hurt in her face not even close to matching the hurt in his heart.

CHAPTER THIRTY SEVEN

Genevieve stood alone on the ramparts of the castle, staring out over the countryside, and she wept. She had never felt so overwhelmed by her emotions, had never felt such a mix of feelings: joy at seeing Royce's face again, and agony and despair at seeing the look of betrayal on his face. That look had shattered her heart. It was a look she would carry with her the rest of her days, a look of such accusation, such despair.

Such betrayal.

If only she'd had one minute to explain to him, to tell him what she was doing and why—to tell him that it had all been for him.

Yet there had been no time. He'd run off into the crowd, and as she'd watched him go, her heart tearing to pieces, she did not know which was more painful: seeing him there in the first place, in that horrible situation, fighting in the Pits, or watching him disappear yet again.

Genevieve stood there, weeping, and as she studied the countryside, she wished she could go back and change everything. What she wouldn't give for one minute with him, one minute to explain everything.

But it was too late now. Royce was gone—and probably this time forever.

The Duke had taken up arms, intent on finding Royce and avenging his dead father. He had assembled a small army, and he and his men were out for blood. Local nobles and lords were flocking to him from all over the region, helping to hunt Royce down. There would be nowhere for Royce to escape. Indeed, as Genevieve looked out, she could see them in the distance, galloping across the countryside in small groups, spreading out, barking dogs at their sides. They sounded horns periodically, and each horn was like a knife in her heart.

Genevieve wondered how it would all end. If only she could have changed things somehow, done something differently. Had she made a mistake? She had thought that becoming a noble would help Royce. But perhaps she had been wrong. What good had it done him, after all? She could not even help free his brothers.

Better, she realized now, to have never ventured down this road. To have never gone to Altfor's chamber. To have never seen

172

Royce again under these circumstances. At least then, their last glance would have been one of pure love; at least their love would have ended on a perfect note.

Now it was soiled, the entire thing ruined.

Genevieve walked to the edge of the balcony, leaned over, and saw how far the fall was. Her heart pounded in her chest. With Royce gone, what did she have left to live for?

This time, she would do it.

Genevieve gripped the marble rail and began to pull herself up, preparing to jump—when suddenly there came the sound of footsteps running behind her.

Genevieve spun and was startled to see a messenger running, frantic, toward her. Heaving, he held out a scroll, gasping for breath as he tried to convey his message.

"My...lady," he gasped. "Where is the Duke? I have an urgent message for him and his men. It concerns Royce."

Upon hearing that word, Genevieve froze. It was the one word that could bring her back from the brink.

She faced him, trembling inside.

"And what is it that concerns Royce?" she asked slowly, her words deliberate, forcing herself to remain calm.

"He's been...spotted," the messenger continued. "In the eastern ridge of the Northern Wood. I must convey this information to the Duke before it's too late!"

Genevieve's heart pounded as she had a sudden realization: she could still be of help to Royce. If she were dead, it would do no good to anyone. Perhaps it was not too late after all. Perhaps she had made the right choice, entering this family of nobles. If it were for only this one moment, it had all been worth it. She was being given a second chance. It was an act of grace, like an angel swooping down to save her from herself.

Genevieve stepped toward the messenger calmly, reached out, and took the scroll. She looked down and examined it; it was heavier than she'd expected, and sealed with wax. It felt good to hold it in her hand.

"I am on my way to see the Duke now," she said coolly, "and I shall give it to him personally."

His face collapsed in relief. He bowed.

"Thank you, Duchess."

He turned and ran off, disappearing back into the fort.

Genevieve broke the seal, opened the scroll, and read it. It was as he'd said. She knew that her hiding this message from the Duke would be on pain of death. If she were ever discovered, she would be hung up and tortured and killed. And she knew that one day, somehow or other, the Duke would find out what she had done. That a messenger had come for him with the news. That she had intercepted the scroll.

One day there would be a reckoning, and she would lose her life.

But that day was not today.

Genevieve turned back to the countryside, held the scroll out over the rail, and slowly, one piece at a time, she tore it to pieces.

It felt good. She watched the pieces fall, sprinkling down on the countryside, taking the very fall that she herself had almost taken, and piece by piece, she felt her heart begin to mend. Finally, she could sacrifice for Royce, too.

Royce, she thought, *I love you.*

ONLY THE VALIANT
(The Way of Steel—Book Two)

"Morgan Rice did it again! Building a strong set of characters, the author delivers another magical world. ONLY THE WORTHY is filled with intrigue, betrayals, unexpected friendship and all the good ingredients that will make you savor every turn of the pages. Packed with action, you will read this book on the edge of your seat."
--Books and Movie Reviews, Roberto Mattos

From Morgan Rice, #1 Bestselling author of THE QUEST OF HEROES (a free download with over 1,000 five star reviews), comes a riveting new fantasy series.

In ONLY THE VALIANT (The Way of Steel—Book Two), Royce, 17, is on the run, fleeing for his freedom. He reunites with the peasant farmers as he attempts to rescue his brothers and flee for good.

Genevieve, meanwhile, learns a shocking secret, one that will affect the rest of her life. She must decide whether to risk her own life to save Royce's—even as he thinks she betrayed him.

The aristocracy prepares for war against the peasantry, and only Royce can save them. But Royce's only hope lies in his secret powers—powers he is not even sure he has.

ONLY THE VALIANT weaves an epic tale of friends and lovers, of knights and honor, of betrayal, destiny and love. A tale of valor, it draws us into a fantasy world we will fall in love with, and appeals to all ages and genders.

Book #3 in the series—ONLY THE DESTINED—is now also available for pre-order.

Books by Morgan Rice

OLIVER BLUE AND THE SCHOOL FOR SEERS
THE MAGIC FACTORY (Book #1)
THE ORB OF KANDRA (Book #2)
THE OBSIDIANS (Book #3)

THE INVASION CHRONICLES
TRANSMISSION (Book #1)
ARRIVAL (Book #2)
ASCENT (Book #3)
RETURN (Book #4)

THE WAY OF STEEL
ONLY THE WORTHY (Book #1)
ONLY THE VALIANT (Book #2)
ONLY THE DESTINED (Book #3)

A THRONE FOR SISTERS
A THRONE FOR SISTERS (Book #1)
A COURT FOR THIEVES (Book #2)
A SONG FOR ORPHANS (Book #3)
A DIRGE FOR PRINCES (Book #4)
A JEWEL FOR ROYALS (BOOK #5)
A KISS FOR QUEENS (BOOK #6)
A CROWN FOR ASSASSINS (Book #7)
A CLASP FOR HEIRS (Book #8)

OF CROWNS AND GLORY
SLAVE, WARRIOR, QUEEN (Book #1)
ROGUE, PRISONER, PRINCESS (Book #2)
KNIGHT, HEIR, PRINCE (Book #3)
REBEL, PAWN, KING (Book #4)
SOLDIER, BROTHER, SORCERER (Book #5)
HERO, TRAITOR, DAUGHTER (Book #6)
RULER, RIVAL, EXILE (Book #7)
VICTOR, VANQUISHED, SON (Book #8)

KINGS AND SORCERERS
RISE OF THE DRAGONS (Book #1)
RISE OF THE VALIANT (Book #2)

THE WEIGHT OF HONOR (Book #3)
A FORGE OF VALOR (Book #4)
A REALM OF SHADOWS (Book #5)
NIGHT OF THE BOLD (Book #6)

THE SORCERER'S RING
A QUEST OF HEROES (Book #1)
A MARCH OF KINGS (Book #2)
A FATE OF DRAGONS (Book #3)
A CRY OF HONOR (Book #4)
A VOW OF GLORY (Book #5)
A CHARGE OF VALOR (Book #6)
A RITE OF SWORDS (Book #7)
A GRANT OF ARMS (Book #8)
A SKY OF SPELLS (Book #9)
A SEA OF SHIELDS (Book #10)
A REIGN OF STEEL (Book #11)
A LAND OF FIRE (Book #12)
A RULE OF QUEENS (Book #13)
AN OATH OF BROTHERS (Book #14)
A DREAM OF MORTALS (Book #15)
A JOUST OF KNIGHTS (Book #16)
THE GIFT OF BATTLE (Book #17)

THE SURVIVAL TRILOGY
ARENA ONE: SLAVERSUNNERS (Book #1)
ARENA TWO (Book #2)
ARENA THREE (Book #3)

VAMPIRE, FALLEN
BEFORE DAWN (Book #1)

THE VAMPIRE JOURNALS
TURNED (Book #1)
LOVED (Book #2)
BETRAYED (Book #3)
DESTINED (Book #4)
DESIRED (Book #5)
BETROTHED (Book #6)
VOWED (Book #7)
FOUND (Book #8)
RESURRECTED (Book #9)

About Morgan Rice

Morgan Rice is the #1 bestselling and USA Today bestselling author of the epic fantasy series THE SORCERER'S RING, comprising seventeen books; of the #1 bestselling series THE VAMPIRE JOURNALS, comprising twelve books; of the #1 bestselling series THE SURVIVAL TRILOGY, a post-apocalyptic thriller comprising three books; of the epic fantasy series KINGS AND SORCERERS, comprising six books; of the epic fantasy series OF CROWNS AND GLORY, comprising eight books; of the epic fantasy series A THRONE FOR SISTERS, comprising eight books (and counting); of the new science fiction series THE INVASION CHRONICLES, comprising four books; of the new fantasy series OLIVER BLUE AND THE SCHOOL FOR SEERS, comprising three books (and counting); and of the new epic fantasy series THE WAY OF STEEL, comprising three books (and counting). Morgan's books are available in audio and print editions, and translations are available in over 25 languages.

Morgan loves to hear from you, so please feel free to visit www.morganricebooks.com to join the email list, receive a free book, receive free giveaways, download the free app, get the latest exclusive news, connect on Facebook and Twitter, and stay in touch!